MURDER IN THE WILLETT FAMILY

THE LT. VALCOUR SERIES

Murder by the Clock
Somewhere in This House
Murder by Latitude
Murder in the Willet Family
Murder on the Yacht
Valcour Meets Murder
The Lesser Antilles Case
Profile of a Murder
The Case of the Constant God
Crime of Violence
Murder Masks Miami

MURDER IN THE WILLETT FAMILY

RUFUS KING

A Lt. Valcour Mystery

WILDSIDE PRESS

For more information, contact:
Wildside Press LLC
www.wildsidepress.com

CHAPTER 1

"*Kill?*"

The commissioner of the New York police force stressed the word gently and stared across pale roses, in a bowl on his desk, at Mrs. Willett. She was lending an air of impeccable austerity even to the flowing lines of the comfortable chair in which she sat, and corsets, the commissioner decided were what did it. Not the new kind, but the old kind that went out twenty years ago—was it?—stuffed hour glasses. He thought of them as a clamp that had kept the years as well as her anatomy rigid. But then she had set at forty, the way plaster of Paris sets, and that had been twenty years ago.

He saw the same over-large and compelling eyes—a Victoria before the sags—much tighter all over than that mellow queen: her cheeks, her chin, the flesh beneath her prominent eyes, all mottled firmness. Even the hair then (twenty years ago, when he had last seen her) had been gray. And the clothes—styles touched Mrs. Willett and left her, to return to her rigid unchangingness and touch her again. Her hats, of course, had always been royal crown made of satins or felts—mitres, maybe—or were those the things one carried in one's hand? He hoped she wasn't going to cry…that moisture edging lazily into her eyes…

He said: "I really don't believe, Kate, in view of what you've told me, that it is as serious as that," while twenty years were so much celluloid touched by fire, and there she was, just as she had been, while he—well, a mirror on a facing wall was not unflattering. "Kidnapping—extortion—yes, but kill? How old are they now?"

"Henry is eighteen and Arthur nineteen. They are very," Mrs. Willett, from practiced usage, chose the word unerringly, "young for their ages."

The commissioner stepped around the statement carefully. He had heard, at moments during those twenty intervening years, certain anecdotes in which Arthur and Henry… He would have preferred delicacy, but wasn't that desirable quality more frequently found, he reflected, in being blunt? "Are you certain that they couldn't have written the message themselves?" he said.

Mrs. Willett grew stiffer within her stiffness, and her eyes, which normally carried a wounded look, were vague with reproaches. "Their humor doesn't take that form, John."

"Of course, Kate—"

It was her old trick, this shocked reproachfulness, when anyone hinted at possible imperfection in anything of hers: a protective cloak, very strong for all its visual frailness, with which she covered her family's little weaknesses; curious little weaknesses, flourishing with impudent and exotic comfort behind this ever-worn cloak of hers. Her darling husband, Allenby Mortimer Willett—that occasionally capering, immaculately whiskered social figure of a past decade, belching his way through eighteen-course dinners, and out of an embassy—his life had been a series of scamperings behind that cloak of Kate's. Allenby was dead now for fifteen years and, the commissioner mentally added, at last.

She left his, "Of course, Kate—" where he had left it, hanging in the air, and began to smooth tight-fitting gloves of glacéed brown kid over large knuckles. "I have many things to do," she said.

"Don't hurry, Kate." He kept staring at her as if she were a knife that had sliced, from his middle, twenty years, and then spliced the gap together again, making him just so much shorter in youngness. "You're never in the city any more."

Lids, like ivory-toned, smooth china, scooped over her eyes. "We never stay very long," she said, "in the same places."

"But I don't ever hear of you!"

"We are a good deal abroad, John, in the odder corners, and when we are here we are very quiet." Her eyes were at him again. "Our life is quite simple—quite quiet. You must appreciate what a shock…"

"You have the messages with you, Kate?"

"I burned them. They said to."

He looked at her curiously. She had always puzzled him, even during those far earlier days when, as youngsters, he had been her guest in her family's great house at Tuxedo. The picture was vividly clear: hillsides sheeted with snow (the visits had always occurred during winter vacations), with her legs in black wool stockings and two pigtails flying from under a round, elastic-fastened hat. Little Kate. Never, never could this woman have been little Kate. "That was foolish. You should have brought them to me at once. We have a department which specializes in extortion cases and, with luck, the letters would have been traced in a week and their sender arrested. The matter would be closed by now."

The quiet efficiency of his voice—its mature decisiveness—she remembered when it used to break. It had seemed so excruciatingly funny, as things can be when you are little—that silly giggling period when

John's voice used to break. Her eyes were heavy with tiredness. She stared over the desk at him. She was wrong. They had never giggled—not he and she; what nonsense it was that could come stabbing out of the past. She said: "I do not think as clearly as I used to."

She was doing it again—using her strange ability at disarmingness. He felt unreasonably angry with her—angry at what must have been the wastedness of all her middle years. She had become during them quite a prominent sportswoman, and had identified herself with several of the more important hunts both in this country and in England. Allenby Mortimer Willett. The name in itself should have constituted a warning. "It wasn't friendly of you not to, Kate."

She said: "You don't know."

Amazing, he thought, what could be wrapped up into three short words—tons of things that he didn't know—all that big stretch of middleness in the life of a person whom, those very many years ago, he had known so well. It fenced her in so (this ignorance of his about those things) and he could only stare at her through palings.

"What were the postmarks?" he said.

"New York. They were all from New York."

"Just how many, Kate?"

"Three."

He kept the gravity that he felt about the business carefully out of his voice. There was no use in adding further alarm to her obvious condition of unease. He recognized very keenly that there was cause for alarm. The Middle West was getting a dose of it—this almost syndicated extortion business. There was no reason why it should not have reached out toward the wealth which cluttered up the East. He leaned forward and smelled one of the yellow roses. "For how long will you want this protection?"

"We will be in the Adirondacks for a week. How straight your shoulders still are, John."

He smiled faintly. "And after that?"

Mrs. Willett shrugged. "After that? Just on, and on."

"Don't you ever get tired? Why don't you settle down again and lead the sort of life you used to? What's wrong with Hillvale, or the town house? Don't the boys ever get tired?"

He felt this careful stepping about after words. "No, the boys never get tired," she said.

He pushed hard against the past; shoved it back into its stifled vagueness. "Look here, Kate, you know perfectly well you can have the best man I've got, but after all he can't be constantly with you. It would mean just one more string attached to my scalp by the taxpayers. They're a public official's private nightmare, the taxpayers. You're a resident, of course, and the threats were mailed here in New York, so we have got a plank to stand on, but what about after this week in the Adirondacks? You say yourself that you're going to keep moving all over. I could recommend the finest sort of a—well, call it a bodyguard if you like, from one of the private agencies."

Mrs. Willett stood up. Her eyes were queer. "I prefer for this week to have someone official," she said.

"But he wouldn't be, Kate. Don't you see? Not up there. What's the county? Essex? Clinton? I don't know the Adirondack counties, but no man from us would have any standing."

"Couldn't he have? I am sure you can arrange it."

(…white-sheeted hillsides—flying legs—snowballs—shrieks—warm and excited lips whispering…) "He could work through the sheriff's office. I could get him deputized, I imagine."

"Then you will, John?"

"You know that I'd never refuse you anything, Kate." He was standing, too; a curious restraint, almost formality, thinned over his genuine friendliness.

"I should prefer, John, someone who has tact."

"The man I am planning to send to you has tact, and is a gentleman."

Mrs. Willett placed her gloved fingertips fleetingly in his hand. "Then take care of him when I return him to you," she said. "There are so few of them left."

The same scent of violets—drifting from sealskin—the same wounded-looking eyes—the utter lack of any parting smile on lips which, from unfamiliarity, had lost that easy art…

"Send me," he said to the policeman who came into the room after she had gone, "Valcour."

CHAPTER 2

The camp which Allenby Mortimer Willett had built in a remote section of seven hundred and fifty acres of mountain, timber, and streams in the Adirondacks was a pretentious affair.

Its main building was a one-story log structure shaped like a T. A miserably dark and oak-timbered hallway ran lengthwise through the center of the T's stem. At the hall's rear end was a door opening onto a broad and unrailed veranda that circuited the whole building.

Along the hallway toward the front, the first door on the right opened into a guest room. This was the room occupied by Lieutenant Valcour during the three wretched days of the first murder and the subsequent inquest. A second guest room was directly across the hall on the left.

Henry and Arthur Willett, and young Wilbur Strange, had the bedroom next after Valcour's, and Mrs. Willett's room was opposite them, on the hall's left.

The hypnotic symmetry of its arrangement was then broken, on the right side of the hallway, by the architect's, under Allenby Mortimer Willett's insistence, having introduced a butler's bedroom (with no door opening into the hallway, but with one into its private bathroom, one to the veranda, and one to an adjoining kitchen), a kitchen, and a pantry. The only entrance from the central hall to these quarters was a door into the kitchen. This door was to assume special importance as it was through it, undoubtedly, that the criminal must have passed after the murder of Arthur.

Finishing up on the left side of the hall were two bedrooms. The first, coming after Mrs. Willett's, was used by Jess and Linda Willett, and the second one by Mrs. Willett's nephew, Larry Stone. The hall itself ended in a door which opened into the great living room.

It was a large room, rectangular in shape (the T had stopped being a stem and had broadened out into its crossbar) with the inevitable huge stone fireplace at its left end. In the front wall was the great entrance door with its iron hinges and its oak bar fastener, while opening out of the right wall were two rooms: the dining room, which was a good-sized square, and a smaller room, called (because it had a case of them in it) the gun room.

With the exception of a cement-lined cellar for the furnace and water system, built under the kitchen and pantry and arrived at by means of a trap-door in the kitchen floor, that ended the main camp building. All of the bedrooms had large cupboards, vapor heat, baths, and no electric lights. Candlelight throughout was the single sop of authenticity which Allenby Mortimer Willett had flung to any backward movement toward nature. Near the main building a large outbuilding served as a garage and servants' quarters, and the permanent caretaker's house stood about an eighth of a mile away.

Bunched cones on the living room hearth were live redness with rich breaths of pine, and Valcour's white shirt front was a stiff amber pool in the couch's deep recess. He stared thoughtfully at Larry Stone, who was sitting at the couch's further end, and dropped ash from his cigarette into a pewter tray on a long table placed flush with the couch's low back. The Navajo chief's rug on the table top held heaven-knew-what wickedness of design: blood, lashing gray creams in pulsing, pine-smelling light... He was curious about Larry Stone. The succinct description of the Willett family, which the commissioner had given him, had been too succinct, and it had not included this nephew of Mrs. Willett's whom he had just met.

Larry had introduced himself, shaken hands, and had sat down. "Where's everybody?" he said.

Valcour smiled. "Who is everybody? I only reached here about three quarters of an hour ago, and I've been dressing since then. So far I've only met you."

"We're six—thank you, Slade."

Larry took a cocktail glass from the tray that Slade was offering him and picked a round of thin toast spread with caviar from a plate of appetizers. Valcour took a cocktail, too. He liked the looks of Slade. The man was a good example of the better class of English upper servant— slender, elderly, with a certain dignity that went a good deal deeper than the merely professional, and an assurance of his trade that had been bred in him from generations.

Slade went away with the tray and Valcour again turned to Larry Stone, whose slight pallor and faint unsteadiness of fingers when he raised the cocktail glass to his lips were contradictory both to his physical build and youth. "There are six of you in the family?" he said.

"Yes, Mr. Valcour. Of course Wilbur's almost one of the family. Wilbur Strange. He'd make us seven."

"Who is Mr. Strange?"

Larry's tone was quite steady. It was the spacing between the words that made them seem on guard to Valcour. "He is a companion for the boys."

"Boys?"

"Arthur and Henry." Larry carefully lighted a cigarette. "We always speak of them as the 'boys.' It has no reference to their ages. They're young men, really."

"They have a brother who is considerably older, haven't they?"

"Jess? Oh, yes. Jess is married—got married last month. I guess Jess is around forty. The Willetts don't keep very good track of ages."

Valcour said suddenly: "Tell me, Mr. Stone, are you aware of the purpose of my being up here?"

"Yes, Mr. Valcour."

"Then do you think that Mrs. Willett's choice was wise?"

"Her choice?"

"Yes. In coming up here where there are so many avenues of approach."

"But there aren't—that's just it. It's why I suggested she come. The road you came along, after you branched off the concrete at the Forks—that's the only safe approach." Larry added, after an imperceptible pause, "For strangers."

"Well, I'm not very familiar with wildernesses, but it does seem as if the forest, pressing almost up to the doors..." Valcour laughed and said: "With each tree hiding its Indian." Even the mild glow from the cocktail hadn't effaced it—a strange sensing of something that was waiting—inimical—in the shadows of this ember-filtered room. Nothing you could touch or see. But the way it is in lush dark vegetation beneath which reptiles with their patience, and their poison, would lie waiting. The thin, clear, pine smell from red cones on the hearth was a drug... "This is why," he continued with an effort, "I have always admired, so, Canada's mounted police."

Larry's, "Because they always get their man?" was dipped in cynicism.

"Well, yes. Don't they?"

"They do because they can't miss him. Look here, Mr. Valcour, there isn't a cop on a New York beat who hasn't a harder job than they have."

"Oh, come now!"

"It's a fact. I'm not speaking about the physical difficulties they have to contend with. They get their man, I tell you, because they can't help getting him. You can sec for yourself that up there in the Northwest there arc only a certain well-tabulated number of places where a fugitive can go—directions—trails he can take. The wilderness itself is a trap for him. I bet you could put a circle around any of the Fifties and Ninth Avenue and find more good hideouts to the square inch than in—"

"Riding your hobby, dear Larry? This is Mr. Valcour, is it not?"

Mrs. Willett was merging toward them from the room's outer darkness, seeping into the glow that spread from the foot of the hearth. The men stood up, and Valcour stared at her curiously while being presented—at her smooth drawn silver hair, arranged at the back in a complicated bun—the low bodice of a maroon-toned velvet dress that gripped her hips and then, indifferently, found its way to the floor—the heavy lace from shoulder straps to elbows, masking thinning arms—the beetle brooch in lapis and rather priceless square-cut emeralds. "Our life up here, Mr. Valcour," she was saying, "is really very simple. I hope you will be able to adjust yourself to it for the week. Mountains—pines—a singularly agreeable stillness and, for us, certain unforgettable and happy memories of past years. We have traps, if stool-shooting interests you. We are all of us quite proficient. Perhaps we can arrange a contest." She accepted a cocktail, which Larry had brought from the tray left by Slade on the table, and sipped it. Her prominent eyes, as they caught those of Valcour, grew sharply informative. "I must see you at once—at once!" he felt he could read in them.

"Where's the rest of the crew, Kate?"

"The boys? There was a little trouble about Arthur's tie. They're coming with Wilbur presently."

Slade was approaching them. He stopped at the glow's discreet fringe. "Dinner is served, madam."

"In a moment, Slade."

"Yes, madam."

"Larry, see if you can help Wilbur about Arthur's tie."

"Right, Kate."

Larry was gone. Slade was gone. And Mrs. Willett stood quite still before the hearth and sipped her cocktail and faced Valcour. "Arthur," she said, "has decided to wear a green tie with his Tuxedo."

Valcour's smile was pleasantly impersonal. "Why not? I think the whole world is going individual, don't you?"

Mrs. Willett vaguely probed the shadows. "They're so full of pranks," she said. "Just like dear Allenby."

"Their father?"

"Their father. Did you know that prankishness was a heritable trait?"

Why didn't she, Valcour wondered, get down at once to what she really wanted to say? "Not exactly. I have usually thought of it as a hang-over."

"From youth?"

"Yes."

"Perhaps it is—thank you." She gave him the empty cocktail glass and he placed it on the table. She fumbled in her bodice and drew out a folded sheet of paper. She said: "There has been another."

Valcour took the paper from her and smoothed it. The side he looked at was quite bare of any writing or of any mark. He turned it over and the other side was quite bare, too. "This?" he said.

"Yes." Mrs. Willett was obviously nervous. Her speaking was rapid. "You appreciate the significance of the message, Mr. Valcour?"

"Message?"

"The one you have just read."

"This sheet of paper is blank, Mrs. Willett."

"The light is uncertain by the fire. Bring it over to this sconce."

Candlelight was whitely yellow on bare paper.

"I'm afraid, Mrs. Willett, that there is nothing here." Valcour looked at her for a moment before adding, "What should there be?"

"One word, Mr. Valcour—'Soon.'"

He returned the paper to her. "You will see that there is nothing there."

She stared at it. "The ink has been chemically treated," she said.

"May I have that paper, please?"

He took it from her and held it slantwise to the light. His eyes were thoughtful. He placed the paper in his pocket. "How did this come to you, Mrs. Willett?"

"In the afternoon mail."

"You still have the envelope?"

"I believe so. I think it is in the basket in my room."

"Did you notice the postmark?"

"Yes. It came from New York. They have all come from New York."

"Have you had it with you all the time, since the moment when you took it out of the envelope?"

"The letter? It was on my dresser, I think, while I was bathing."

"Your bathroom adjoins your dressing room?"

"Yes, but the door—" The sentence died out in stillness. Her eyes were arrested sharply in their ceaseless probing. For an instant they caught and held Valcour's, and then went back again to where the room was darkest. "Henry? You're standing over there aren't you, dear?" Her voice was suddenly brisk. "Come over here, child. I want you to meet Mr. Valcour." Henry made no sound as he came over and stood beside them. He shook hands with Valcour. His grip was uncertain. His hair was coarse and gave the effect of just having been smoothed of knots. He had

Mrs. Willett's prominent eyes, but there was a faint lack of clarity about them.

"Arthur," Henry said, "is wearing a green tie." An odd quality about his laugh made it almost a giggle.

Mrs. Willett was smoothing his hair, her fingers moving restlessly over its coarseness. "Will he be long, dear?"

Henry shook his head impatiently from the stroking, large-knuckled fingers and came closer to Valcour, his legs apart, his hands restlessly jiggling in his trouser pockets. "I say, Valcour, what did the Giants do to-day?"

"I've been traveling since morning. I haven't had a chance to see a baseball edition. Do you get the papers up here, Mrs. Willett?" Valcour turned to her, and Henry shifted his position too, until the unclear eyes were again staring straight at him. They were uncanny, those eyes. There was something not normal about them.

"No, we don't," Henry said. "We don't get a beastly thing up here in this beastly place. Even the radio's a battery set—Here, I'll show you."

He caught Valcour by an arm and dragged him toward a darker corner where a radio stood; then tubes warmed up and a grating loud-speaker harshly mutilated music from the Ritz in Montreal, tearing the dark stillness loudly, drowning Mrs. Willett's, "Dear boy—a little lower, darling."

"Rotten, isn't it?" shouted Henry, and Mrs. Willett descended on them in a dark maroon velvet cloud, and was turning the switch until silence drenched them like clear cold water.

Valcour felt his eyes drawn toward the fireplace. Two figures had come in during the racket and were standing on the hearth. One of them was the counterpart of Henry, except for a bright green tie; the other one was a heavy shaft of stolid sullenness, with muscles pressing the cloth of a well-cut dinner suit.

"I say, Mother," Henry was shouting, "look at Arthur. Arthur's got a cocktail. I'm going to have one, too—come on, there, Valcour, and watch me drink a cocktail."

Henry's fingers were dragging him back to the fire, and Valcour caught a black flash in the dull, coal-colored eyes of the sullen young man beside Arthur.

"Mr. Strange, Mr. Valcour," Mrs. Willett said. "And this is dear Arthur."

Valcour bowed, and a sudden voice at his left elbow made him turn sharply—"Mr. Valcour? I think we're the last of the tribe. I'm Jess—Jess Willett—and this is Linda who recently, in a moment of weakness, became my wife."

Jess's voice hovered about Boston, and Valcour shook hands with this elder brother. Jess's grip was hard. Jess was big. There was a sleepy, magnetic, physical force about him, as there is about certain animals—nothing of the leopard—nothing sleek—more of the bear cub—and he looked much younger than his forty years. Valcour turned from him to Linda. It was Linda's incredible beauty that struck him at once—pale flesh out of soft white satin, with smooth blonde hair cupping wide and frightened eyes. Her fingertips were cold.

"I say, this beastly shaker's empty." Ice rattled hollowly as Henry shook it.

"One is enough, dear boy."

"But Arthur had two. You did, didn't you. Arthur? You beastly little sneak."

"Henry, darling!"

"Let him stew, Mother." Arthur's voice was shrill. "Polecat!"

"I'm not."

"You are, you beast. He is—"

Linda's, "Dear God!" came to Valcour thinly as a reed note dying in dissonant brasses, and Larry Stone came suddenly into the room and said to Mrs. Willett loudly: "When do we eat, Kate?"

Mrs. Willett placed her fingertips on Valcour's arm and kept them there as they started from the room. Henry clung to his other arm and walked staring up at him with Mrs. Willett's doglike eyes, and saying importantly, "I'm going to sit beside you, Valcour, because I like you."

"And I'm going to sit beside Linda," Arthur said, hanging onto Linda's cold, frightened hand, and adding, "because she's pretty. Jess's pretty Linda. Jess has pretty Linda." Then giggling—giggling—giggling—while bunched cones on the hearth were live redness with rich breaths of pine and the room, quite emptied of its people, was remarkably still.

CHAPTER 3

The piano in the living room was definitely out of tune.

Valcour stood near it and looked down at Linda, at her white, cold, nervous fingers jiggling its dissonant keys, while in the room's center five chairs were arranged with their sides touching, their backs alternating and, circling around them, the others were playing "Going to Jerusalem"—Mrs. Willett breathing from over-exertion—the boys pushing, hesitating, clutching chair backs, giggling hysterically—Wilbur Strange unsmiling and stolid beneath coal-colored eyes—Larry methodically antic, and Jess, his face full-bloodedly red, doing it rather seriously, quite eager to win. Linda's cold white fingers tinkled out the threadbare tune, stopped abruptly, and Mrs. Willett (who always arranged it that way) was left without a chair and could go to the couch and sit down. The boys shrieked, and a chair was removed, and cold white fingers were tinkling again—tinkling—tinkling…heavy breathing…feet shuffling bare boards…

"Do they do this every evening?" Valcour said.

Linda did not look up at him. "Every evening. They have for years."

"You've known the family for a long while?"

"I met the family after my wedding last month."

The tinkle stopped for more screaming, and Larry Stone joined Mrs. Willett on the couch, and the boys and Jess and young dark Wilbur Strange were circling again warily, swinging around the ends like whips. The music stopped and there were two chairs and the three brothers left, and at the next stop there were Jess and Henry and only one chair left. Arthur was sulking near Wilbur Strange's armchair because he had lost, and Linda was mechanically tinkling, then suddenly looking up at Valcour and saying, "They take it *seriously*."

"Because it's play. Take sport, take your Olympics, surely you know they take those games seriously—so much so that people are always on the point of starting a war about them, a war which can be pleasantly enjoyed—unseriously."

"But Jess—" The tune went tinkling on, and her voice was a whisper drowned in it. "I want you to look at Jess's face." There was nothing astonishing to Valcour in Jess's face. His earlier impression of a bear cub with a Boston accent remained. "That's from habit," he said. "You'd look just like that, too, if you'd been doing the same thing at a certain hour in the same way for a good many years."

Her, "Will I?" was drenched with a violent discord and her fingers, as she placed them momentarily on Valcour's hand, were dry ice. She said, "Well, I won't—I won't—" but her voice was lost in the infernal racket that Henry was making because he and Jess were both sitting on the final chair. He was trying to push Jess off and, "Cheat! Cheat!" he was yelling at the top of his lungs.

"You can't cheat at this game, young man," Jess said, and shoved steadily back against Henry's frenzy.

"It is a tie, darling. I'm sure you'll concede that it is a tie?" Mrs. Willett was standing, holding ringed fingers out in a general appeal to the others to back her decision.

"He pushed me in my stomach."

"You know where liars go to, youngster."

"You did—he did."

"I'll whale you good and proper if you say that again."

"You and who else? You and who else?" Henry started to giggle in self-appreciation of the antique come-back. "I say there, Valcour, didn't this beast push me in my stomach?" Quite suddenly young Wilbur Strange was standing over Henry, touching him lightly on the shoulder, and saying: "It is time for checkers."

Henry looked up at him oddly. "All right," he said.

Then Arthur was across the room and dragging at Linda. "And I'll beat Linda. Come on, Linda, I'll beat you two straight out of three. You're an awful dub at checkers, and I can beat you any time I like."

Linda's face was frostbitten. "I don't think tonight…" her lips were saying.

"I'll play with you, dear.' Mrs. Willett's fingers were at Arthur's blond hair, stroking it, smoothing its knotted look.

"I don't want you to. Linda's pretty."

Mrs. Willett didn't flinch, exactly. Her look at Valcour was meant to say: there is nothing to understand, it is quite all right. She did say: "Just like his dear father—a perfect eye for beauty. It was the single feminine attribute with which dear Allenby found no complaint."

Linda clung with one white-knuckled hand to the piano seat while Arthur was tugging at the other.

"I'm tired—I've got a headache," she said.

Larry joined them and said to Arthur: "Linda's tired. She's got a headache. How about taking me on instead? God knows I'm not beautiful, but I'm wicked at checkers."

"All right." Arthur dropped Linda's hand and stuck his tongue out at her. "See if I care," he said.

Linda was standing and looking uncertainly from Mrs. Willett to Jess. "I really have a headache. Do you mind?"

She started walking toward the door which led to the bedrooms. Jess waited sleepily until she had almost reached it, and then went over to her and said something. Jess followed her out into the darkened hallway and shut the door, and after a moment it opened again and Jess came back into the room with Linda. Her eyes were dead-looking. She went over to the couch and sat down, and Jess went with her. He took her hand in his and consciously held it quite tightly, and was bending back the fingers.

"I wish you wouldn't do that, please," she said.

"I know you do."

"But surely you play hearts, Mr. Valcour?" Mrs. Willett was saying.

Valcour took his eyes unwillingly from the couch, from Linda who was a set piece of stone, and from Jess whose hair was rumpled as though a hand had been pushed against it hard. It made Jess look like one of the boys—bigger—cleaner—but still…

"Why, yes, Mrs. Willett, although I haven't played hearts for quite a while."

"I prefer it to the more modern games. Contract does not appeal to me. Bezique, unfortunately, seems to have become a lost art. Bezique was dear Allenby's favorite. You will play?"

"With pleasure." He detained her as she started to move away. "Wouldn't it be wiser, Mrs. Willett, for us first to talk things over?"

"Not here. Not now." Mrs. Willett looked frightened.

He followed her example and kept his voice quite low. "Forgive this persistency, but surely we can go into one of the other rooms and confer?"

"Not now—the boys—the slightest thing upsets them so—if an inkling of all this—" Larry Stone was coming toward them and she spoke rapidly: "I will join you when the boys have gone to bed. They go to bed early—ten."

"Just as you wish."

"Can I mix you a highball, Mr. Valcour?" Larry said.

"Make it a slender one, please."

"Scotch? Rye? Ginger ale? Water?"

"Rye and ginger ale."

"Good God! Never heard of it. Kate?"

"Nothing, dear Larry. Will you join us at hearts?"

"Right, Kate."

"How did the checkers come out? Did Arthur beat you?" Larry laughed shortly. "We haven't been playing."

"No?"

"No."

Valcour followed Larry's eyes to where Arthur was sitting. Arthur's fingers were fumbling about with the checkers, piling them, knocking them down again, but he wasn't looking at the checkers. He was looking at Linda.

Larry went off to get highballs, and Mrs. Willett said forcefully: "The dear child sits that way for hours. He adores the girl. So pretty. The card table is against that wall over there, Mr. Valcour. Shall we set it up? Thank you—no—I think the light is better over here by the couch. I'm sure that Jess and dear Linda will join us. Jess is quite adept at hearts."

Valcour could feel it again: that curious undercurrent of danger. Vague, even as Mrs. Willett was vague. He glanced toward the windows and assured himself that the shades were drawn. Criminal, this waiting. They should, with the first darkening of night, at least have posted one guard… He placed the card table before the couch, and Arthur was with them in a flash, sitting on the other side of Linda from Jess, pressing quite near her, his elbow knocking her whenever he moved jerkily.

From a checker table close by, young dark Wilbur Strange was saying to Henry: "That is two games I've won."

Henry looked sly. "That's only because I lost on purpose," he said.

CHAPTER 4

Arthur was murdered that night.

It was a sharp night, chill, very dry, heavy with pine, and the sky a dark cap, star-crowded, circled by black and uneven tops close-edging the mountain valley.

Mrs. Willett held a short mink cloak about her tight-corseted body, and the high heels of her slippers tapped sharply on the veranda's oak flooring. Her right hand was tense in the crook of Valcour's arm and he waited, as they walked, for her to speak. He sensed her nervous reaction to the impressionable stillness. It came crowding against them from everywhere, this special stillness, out of the star-flecked sky—out of the walls of the mountains—out of the phalanxed trees that were high blacknesses on the fringe of the impudent, shallow clearing.

"Have you ever shielded anyone, Mr. Valcour?" she said.

"In what way, Mrs. Willett?"

"From harm."

"That's rather a blanketing word, isn't it? Do you mean physical harm?"

"I mean all harm, Mr. Valcour."

"I don't think I have."

"Then you will find it difficult to understand what must appear to you to be decided vagaries in my attitude."

He kept quite still, waiting for her to be more explicit. He knew she would come to the point after she had found, by first trying several, the easiest path by which to reach it.

She said: "We are responsible not only to God for our children, but to the children themselves. More so. Children are our flesh and blood. The triteness of that statement will never erase the deep truth of it. We can touch them. They can hurt us. They are real. I see my children, Mr. Valcour, as nobody else could ever see them. I am not blinded to their faults by my love. I see them, each fault, quite clearly, but their possible unpleasantness is diluted in my love." She veered abruptly. "A thing is increasingly precious in ratio to its rarity. Do you know what I have come to think is the most precious thing on earth?"

"Yes, Mrs. Willett?"

"Peace of mind." She then said almost fiercely: "At least some measure of it shall belong to my three sons." A noise in the underbrush made her tremble. It seemed, as she pressed suddenly near to him, as if her whole body were shaking. "An animal," she said.

His eyes were trying to force a way through the thick outer darkness. "Just an animal."

They saw the glow of a cigarette coming toward them from around the corner of the veranda. It was Larry, who came up to them and said, "They've gone to bed."

Larry fell in on the other side of Mrs. Willett. They went to the front door and inside into the living room, where Jess was waiting for them over by the hearth.

It was a strange conference. There was something of strain in the attitude of each of them. Valcour could sense it as his look passed casually from Jess to Mrs. Willett and to Larry Stone. There was a closeness in it, too: a definite closing-in of the three of them into a unit. "Mr. Valcour," Jess said, "we can now decide upon what is best for us to do."

They were patently waiting for him to speak. Mrs. Willett did not sit down. She had her back to the fire, darkly silhouetted against its flame, her skin shadowed ivory against its redness, and her large important-looking eyes deep in violet shade. They grouped near her, Jess very close to her, very much a part of her, and Larry quite close to her, too.

Valcour said: "It is always beneficial to keep a clear-cut picture before one's mind when faced with any problem. The outline which the commissioner gave me is plain: an extortionist has been threatening Mrs. Willett to kidnap her two younger sons unless twenty thousand dollars were handed over in cash. Three letters were sent containing threats, and the third letter in addition contained instructions as to the method for delivering the money." Valcour's manner was quietly matter-of-fact and his eyes, more frequently than on either of the others, rested on Larry Stone, on the faint occasional twitch of facial muscles, as though some inner and dreaded knowledge were chafing beneath an ill-fitting mask. "I understand that Mrs. Willett followed those instructions, and that nothing happened. The rendezvous was not kept. Mrs. Willett wisely conferred with the commissioner and then, upon the advice of Mr. Stone, came up here. Well, we are here."

"What do you make of that letter which Mother got this afternoon, Mr. Valcour?" Jess said.

"Several things would appear to be obvious, Mr. Willett. Its sender knows that you are up here. One could also infer that its sender knew that Mrs. Willett had got in touch with the police and would not destroy that last letter, which came this afternoon, as she had the other three. The fact that the word 'soon' which comprised the message has disappeared might point to that." His eyes kept staring at them curiously. "It interests me that the ink on the envelope that that letter came in, and which Mrs. Willett was fortunate enough to retrieve from her waste basket, did not vanish too."

They offered nothing, said nothing. They stood in their tight little group before the hot, red fire. Then Larry said: "How about it, Mr. Valcour—is there liable to be any immediate danger from all this?"

"Not if the case runs true to form. Extortionists, Mr. Stone, are out after money. That's their main objective. Unless they work in gangs they're a cowardly lot of pretty filthy individuals. Singly, they don't go in very much for violence, except in quite rare instances."

"Then why wasn't this one on hand to get the money?" Larry said. "Kate had it. She was willing enough to pay. That's what gets me."

Valcour's eyes were grave. "It gets me too, Mr. Stone. It is one of the reasons why I feel that we should take some elementary precautions."

Jess said: "Such as, Mr. Valcour?"

"You must have some men on this place who have been with you a good many years, Mr. Willett?"

"Normally we would have, if we were going it full blast. But we're not. Our caretaker's family and Slade are running the whole works. Oscar Moore's the caretaker. Oscar has two sons who are doing the chores—taking care of the furnace—driving the car—things like that. His wife cooks, and his daughter does what housework we need." Jess's voice grew impersonally vague. "We haven't entertained up here much recently. It was different when we did."

"So different, Mr. Valcour." Mrs. Willett's hand closed gently on Jess's, protectively, in an unconscious open gesture of that deep and enduring love which she felt for this eldest son—this first-born—every inch of her body was filled with it, with this love. Jess gave her covering hand a squeeze and then dropped it again. "When we really do open up here, I never know whether I'm running a house or an army. You are suggesting, of course, that we have a guard. Oscar's two sons will do splendidly. Jess will arrange for them to patrol the grounds. They are dependable. Most dependable."

Her lips were whitish, and Valcour wondered what streams of miserable anxiousness were sapping the strength away from under her assured and efficient manner. "That will be satisfactory," he said.

"Is there anything else we can do?" Jess wanted to know.

"I am mailing the envelope and paper which Mrs. Willett got this afternoon to headquarters in the morning. They will be attended to by the proper department. It is our only lead. We must wait."

"I say, Kate," Larry said suddenly, "how about shooting a highball with us and then turning in? Personally I feel like the fourth conspirator from the left in the fifth act of King Lear, and you look like hell."

"Dear boy." She managed one of her rare smiles. "A glass of port. You'll find some crackers in the pantry, too." She said to Valcour: "My strength is not what it used to be when I was young."

Larry went out and after a while came back again carrying a tray with three highballs on it, a plate of crackers, and a glass of port. They sat by the fire and talked and drank their drinks and tried to glaze over by almost mechanical conversation the dread that was putting lead in their hearts. And after they'd finished their drinks Mrs. Willett went off to bed, and Jess and Larry got flashlights and started for the caretaker's house to arrange with Oscar Moore to have his two sons patrol the grounds for the night.

Valcour went to his room. He sat at its desk and wrote (as the commissioner had directed him to) a lengthy and complete report directly to the commissioner himself.

Part of it read:

"There are forces working in this affair that are unusual. Wilbur Strange is a case in point. Mrs. Willett herself is another. We are both of us only too familiar with the muck which any investigation of private lives stirs up. Muck is far too strong a word in this instance. But there are sidelines. Hidden things which I feel will slowly and inevitably rise to the surface. There is a bad situation existing between Jess Willett and his wife. Larry Stone, the nephew, has something preying on his mind. It is either something that he has done, or that he knows. He is keeping it secret, and it is wearing on his nerves. I have nothing definite on which to base my belief, but I do not feel that this is a plain extortion case. It is not as simple as that. I will appreciate a quick report on the enclosed sheet of paper and envelope. They constitute our only starting point, and I urgently believe that there is danger in delay."

Valcour addressed the envelope, sealed it, and put it in his pocket. The glow from the single candle on his desk was feeble and he mentally cursed all back-to-nature poses. Give him, he begged, while opening his suitcase and taking out a flashlight and a flat black automatic, both of which he put in his jacket pocket, a good honest electric light with a button to push when you wanted it. Then he cursed it once more, and blew out the candle.

The hallway was a tunnel of stillness, and in all the building there was no sound at all. A shock of rumpled blond hair showed above the couch's low back when he came into the living room. He thought at first that the hair belonged to one of the hoys. He found out it was Jess, when he reached the couch; Jess, sprawled in a corner of it with his muscular legs shoved straight out, his hands pushed deep in his trouser pockets, his eyes looking rather little, staring at a snapping, loud-crackling, four-foot log he had set on the red pulsing embers. "When does the next mail leave here, Mr. Willett?" he said.

"For the south?"

"Yes."

"Not before noon to-morrow. There's an airmail service from Plattsburg, though, if you're in a hurry about anything."

Valcour sat down on the couch's further end. "Will it be agreeable to take a letter to Plattsburg the first thing in the morning?"

"Quite. Oscar will run you in right after breakfast." Jess looked at a watch on his broad strong wrist. "We fixed it all right about Oscar's sons," he said.

"What reason did you give them, Mr. Willett?"

"I told them that Mother was nervous, Mr. Valcour. They are fond of her. She has done a great deal for that whole family."

Valcour carefully dropped ash from his cigarette into the pewter tray. "Mr. Willett, tell me something about young Strange."

"Wilbur?" Jess's voice was evasive. "Wilbur's all right."

"Where does he come from? Who is he?"

Jess shrugged. "He's in my mother's department, Mr. Valcour. My mother has always been vague in regard to him. My mother can be, and frequently is, a very vague woman." Jess looked at his wrist watch again. His voice changed abruptly—hardened. "The ten minutes are up," he said.

Jess left the couch, and Valcour watched him slouching to the door to the hall. It wasn't slouching, exactly, for every muscle in that compact, stolid body was coordinating fluidly, like slow rippling metal.

"Good-night, Mr. Valcour."

"Good-night, Mr. Willett."

Jess was gone and the door leading to the bedrooms was shut. "The ten minutes are up." What "ten minutes"? Valcour wondered. And what was "up"? Dark emptiness was left him, faintly brightened by one low burned candle in a sconce and by red flame and embers on the noisy hearth. But it wasn't emptiness. There was someone in the room. A threadlike sound of someone quietly creeping through the stillness near the other end of the couch. Valcour's hand slid swiftly into the pocket where he had the gun. He was drawing it out when Arthur's giggle made him release it again, and Arthur was over the end of the couch and sprawled where Jess had just been sprawling, with just the rough mop of his unkempt hair rising above the couch's low back, where Jess's had just been.

"See here, Valcour," Arthur said, "what's this all about?"

"Why were you hiding in this room?" Valcour said, not smiling, and his eyes carefully appraising Arthur's untidy figure, with its loose woolen bathrobe over rumpled flannel pajamas.

"Don't you wish you knew? I say, old man, give me a cigarette."

Valcour opened his case and offered it to Arthur, who reached for it, still sprawling. Arthur stuck the cigarette in his mouth and waited for Valcour to light it. Its end was already wet and loose before the match had touched it.

"Is your brother hiding in here, too?" Valcour said.

"Henry?"

"Yes."

Arthur giggled unpleasantly. "Henry's asleep." The log on the hearth crackled loudly, extravagantly, and showers of hot red sparks fanned blazing up the chimney. "Look here, what are you up here for? What were you talking to Jess about?"

"Didn't you hear?"

"What's all this stuff about Oscar's sons?"

"We were talking over some plans for tomorrow. Where is Mr. Strange?"

Arthur's unnatural giggle was there again. "He's in bed, too." A sudden and petulant anger was in his voice. "Don't be a beast. You and Jess were talking about to-night, about guarding something. What are you up here for, anyway?"

Valcour's eyes were held by fountained sparks. He waited until the hiss of their explosive crackling was quieted in the dim and spaceless room.

"I am up here as a guest of your mother."

The statement was unheeded in the deep still hush, and the flames on the hearth were lazy again, very lazy, very silent again. The silence stretched into a minute. Over the pungent pine smell drifted faintly a smell of burning cloth. Cigarette—sloppily wet and drooping—Valcour dragged his eyes from the hypnotic fire and looked at Arthur. The cigarette lay on Arthur's lap. The smell of burning cloth was stronger. Valcour reached over quickly and slapped the place on Arthur's leg where the cloth was singed and smoldering, and Arthur's hand, loosely lying across a knee, slid loosely to the couch.

"You shouldn't fall asleep with a lighted cigarette in your hand," Valcour said.

Arthur's chin was slumped on his chest. Arthur didn't answer him. Arthur was dead.

CHAPTER 5

There was no pulse. The pupils of Arthur's eyes did not react to match flame. The heart beneath the rumpled pajamas did not beat. This somber darkness… Valcour lighted another of the candle-filled sconces on the table and then quite clearly he could see the back of Arthur's head and in its short, coarse, bristling hair a small dark mark where a bullet had entered and lodged in Arthur's brain.

Valcour stared at the open doorway to the dining room. It was, he judged, about fifty feet from the rear of the couch. He lifted one of the sconces and walked rapidly toward it.

The dining room was empty, but there was a definite smell of cordite in the air. The shot had unquestionably been fired from the vicinity of its doorway. He went through the swinging door into the pantry—empty—through the pantry into the kitchen—empty—but its door opening out onto the veranda was ajar and through it was the black cold night, with darkness and endless cover for a fugitive, while somewhere out in that darkness Oscar Moore's two sons were patrolling… How still the whole house was! He soulfully wished he could call up the nearest precinct station and throw a cordon around the block. But there was no precinct station. There was no block. He opened the door leading into the hallway and stood, for an instant, motionless. Something…of course: when he had left the living room, its door into this hallway had been closed. Valcour was sure of it. And now that door was open. He hurried toward it, stood arrested at it, looking at Linda who was by the end of the couch staring down upon Arthur's dead body. And Wilbur Strange was standing at the couch's other end, and he wasn't looking at the body. He was looking at Linda. "That's one," Wilbur said.

A shudder went through Linda. "He's dead."

Wilbur saw Valcour just then in the doorway. "Do you know about this?" His heavy voice was obviously controlled. "Arthur's dead. He's been killed. He's been shot in the back of the head."

"I know, Mr. Strange. I was with him."

Wilbur started to laugh. Linda's, "Don't—don't, please, you mustn't!" was lost in that hard and unnatural laugh, and Larry Stone came suddenly into the room and said: "What's up? What's the matter here? Stop that damn noise, Wilbur. Look at Arthur—I say—"

"He has been killed, Mr. Stone." Valcour looked steadily at Larry.

Larry's face was chalk. "One of the rare instances, Mr. Valcour," he said.

"Let us hope so. I want you to stay in this room. See that nothing is touched until I get back."

Valcour left them, and Larry stared peculiarly from Linda's shaking body to Wilbur. "Has anybody told Kate?"

Linda's lips said: "I don't think so."

Larry's eyes were boring into her. "Where's Jess?"

"I thought he was in here, Larry." Linda didn't know which was worse: Arthur's dead blank face or Wilbur Strange's contorted and sullen one. "That's why I'm here. I came in here to find him. He wasn't here. Nobody was here but Arthur. Then Wilbur came in here."

"Better sit down, Linda.'"

"I feel all right, thank you, Larry."

"You should."

"What's that?" Larry swung sharply on Wilbur.

"I say she should. One's gone."

"What are you talking about?"

"Ask her."

"You trying to make out that Linda's mixed up in *this*?"

"Well—"

Larry's knuckles were sore from the force of the blow where they struck Wilbur's chin, and Wilbur's tough, stocky body crashed heavily on the floor. Wilbur's eyes stayed open and looked dazed for a moment. Then they cleared and stared up from the floor at Larry.

"Good enough," he said.

Larry helped him to his feet. "Don't talk any rot like that again."

Linda's lower lip was moving the way a rabbit's does when it is caught by the headlights from a car. Nothing else about her body was moving at all. Just that lower lip fluttering. Larry nodded toward Arthur.

"I wonder what's really the answer to this," he said. Wilbur Strange kept sullenly silent, and a few words that Linda spoke were not understandable. "We ought to lay him out flat on the couch."

"I understood Mr. Valcour to say that nothing was to be touched," Wilbur said.

"I know, but we can't let Kate come in and find him this way. She's crazy about him. For God's sake, Linda, get away from here and go sit down."

"I'm all right, Larry."

"What?"

"I say that I'm quite all right." Her voice was stronger and the ice that had frozen tight all through her had melted a little. Larry said suddenly to Wilbur: "Where's Henry?"

"Sleeping, I suppose. He was when I left him."

"And you're sure that Jess isn't in your room, Linda?"

"He wasn't when I left it." Her eyes grew startled, and the bitter chill came back again. "He takes walks. Often he goes out at night and takes walks."

"Yes," Larry said slowly, "I know."

"Jess is the one who should tell her, isn't he, Larry?"

"Kate?"

"Yes. It's so terrible to think of her sleeping in there and not knowing—I mean her having to know—to wake up and be told—"

Valcour came quickly into the room with Slade. There was a touch of disorder in Slade's clothes, in his thinning hair. His lips were as pallid as his face and he kept murmuring on uneven breaths, "Dreadful—dreadful—dreadful."

"Dr. Ferris will be here shortly," Valcour said, as he joined the others at the couch. "I have had the sheriff on the telephone and he told me that Dr. Ferris is the deputy coroner at the Forks. I will ask both of you gentlemen," he said to Larry and to Wilbur Strange, "to take flashlights and assist me in an immediate search of this building and the grounds around it. As the earth is covered with pine needles right up to the veranda, there will be no necessity for guarding against the obliterating of any footprints. Slade will stay in here with the body." He said directly to Linda: "Where is Mr. Willett? Is he in his room?"

Her lip was at it again, and even the nearness of the fire on the hearth couldn't make her stop from feeling that deadly coldness, and suddenly Jess himself was saying from the dining room doorway: "No, I'm not in my room, Mr. Valcour. I'm here." Jess was walking towards where they were standing. Jess was looking down upon Arthur's untidy body and speaking again, saying: "Looks as if it might have been made by a twenty-two. Poor, crazy little tike." Then Jess was coming to her and Linda felt herself pulled roughly into his arms, and his warm strong hotness going through her, melting her, and she didn't care, because all the coldness was leaving her, while she wondered whether she could keep on hating him, and loving him so, and, "What in hell have you been doing to Linda?" he was saying.

"Not a damn thing," Larry said.

"Well, don't."

"Gentlemen, it is advisable that this search be made at once." Valcour's voice was steadying. "You are not familiar with the singularly unpleasant after-effects of a capital crime. Let us do everything that we can to prevent them. I believe that this search will prove futile, but it is one of the routine things that has got to be done." He said to Jess: "Will you please advise your mother, Mr. Willett, about this unfortunate business? I believe it will distress her least in that way. Slade, you will be good enough to stay here and see that nothing at all is touched. Gentlemen, we will start outside."

He went, followed by Larry and Wilbur Strange, onto the front veranda. They were close to him, like sheep in strange pastures. "I will fire several shots into the air," he said, taking out his revolver. "That ought to bring in the two Moore boys who are patrolling. It is possible they may have something to report."

Five shots crashed loudly in the still night air and sharply, from inside the building, came dreadful screams.

"That's Henry," Wilbur Strange said. "I'd better go in to him."

CHAPTER 6

Henry had stopped screaming. He hadn't any voice left him to scream with. He was on his knees in front of Arthur, and Mrs. Willett was on her knees too, with Henry pressed convulsively against her woolen-robed body that was so tired—so old—his head was a puddle of dull molasses against the dressing gown's faded blue.

"Darling—darling—you mustn't *think*," she was saying to him, with strange wet softnesses in her capable voice. "Just close your eyes, my darling, and do not think." But his eyes were closed. They were shut tight while her own, like plummets, stared at Arthur's slumped, dead head.

"Perhaps if you would let me take him, Mrs. Willett?"

She knew it was Wilbur Strange's voice and that he was on one knee at Henry's other side. She pressed Henry's body more tightly to her. "No. Not now. His place is with me." It was incredible that suddenly, so very suddenly, she should feel quite old. She had once heard Jess describe the finish of a long and bitterly contested running race. She found herself remembering that race, remembering the winner of it who, in the unconscious agony of those last few dozen steps… "Will you make Arthur more comfortable?" she said.

Jess said from the other side of the room, where he was with Linda, "We mustn't."

Mrs. Willett stood up. It was a question of getting to her feet, really. Her body was heavy with strange anchors. She made Henry stand up, too. "Mustn't?"

"Mr. Valcour wants nothing touched," Wilbur said.

"Take Henry, please."

"Yes, Mrs. Willett."

She transferred Henry, as a stuffed and inanimate sack, from her own arms into the support of Wilbur Strange. She moved upon the couch… something Spartan…

"Mother—don't!"

Jess's voice was sharp and he was coming toward her, but he did not reach her before Arthur was quite flat and orderly on the couch.

"That is better," she said.

Jess watched her smoothing the still, ungainly hair. "You're letting us in for trouble, Mother."

She paid no attention to him, but went right ahead with what she was doing—little smoothings—as much as she liked; since for ever so long, not since he had been a baby, had she been able to smooth his poor thick hair for as much as she liked—and soon Arthur looked oddly neat and not a bit unpleasant, as he had when he had been alive. Valcour came in and stood near her until she straightened up and saw him.

"I am sorry you have done this."

"You seem to forget, Mr. Valcour, that this is my child."

"Please do not doubt my genuine and deep sympathy for you, Mrs. Willett, but I must impress upon you the gravity of murder. Permit me to be blunt. My own position here is one through courtesy. In consequence, I must observe the forms as well as the spirit of the office to which the sheriff has deputized me all the more strictly. I must ask you to consider me from now on in my official capacity and not as a guest. I hope that Dr. Ferris will understand as well as I do why the body has been moved."

Mrs. Willett's crying was effortless; nothing but wetness that gathered in her large eyes, filled them, and then ran negligently down her expressionless face. "Dr. Ferris is an old friend,' she said.

"I am sincerely glad of that."

"Did you search the building, Mr. Valcour?" Jess had left Linda and was over near them again.

"Yes."

"Whoever did this had left?"

"I found no one in my search."

"Did the Moore boys have anything to report?"

"Nothing."

"Hadn't we better notify the villages to be on the lookout?"

"I have already done so, Mr. Willett, through the sheriff. He is also arranging that the state-trooper patrols, as well as any government patrols in the vicinity, be notified. He will be over here himself in the morning."

Stillness swamped them, to be broken by Wilbur Strange, whose voice, when he spoke, was a faint far-off drum—hollow—deep—almost meaningless: "There was no purpose—no reason to kill him."

"Oh, but there was, there was!" The words coming from Mrs. Willett were a broken rush. "Those dreadful notes—"

Wilbur looked at her blankly. "What notes, Mrs. Willett?"

"The ones I've been getting since August."

"Yes, Mrs. Willett?"

"They've demanded money, or else they were going to kidnap Arthur and Henry."

Henry's scream blasted shockingly. He was at his mother and clutching her arms savagely. "You let them kill Arthur because you won't pay money—you beastly old woman, you'll let them kill me because you won't pay money!" His voice was a grating shout and his lips worked loosely.

"Darling—dear child—my darling—"

"Go away from me. Don't touch me, you beast."

"Shut up." Jess's broad hand cracked across Henry's loose lips. They started to bleed. "Dirty little swipe."

Mrs. Willett had Henry in her arms again, and he was flaccid, a little dazed, and he let her wipe the blood from his lips with her handkerchief; let her press his gangling body to her, too stunned even to shake the large knuckled fingers from stroking his hair. He was frightened.

"Jess hit me," he said.

Mrs. Willett's eyes were overwhelmingly defensive. "The child has never been struck, Mr. Valcour—never touched—he doesn't quite understand."

"I'm going to kill Jess," Henry said.

"Hush, my darling—cry, dear—there—I am taking him to my room, Mr. Valcour." It was a question.

"Certainly, Mrs. Willett. Can we help you?"

Her look settled on Wilbur Strange. "Will you?"

Wilbur went with her, helping her to support Henry, whose crying was unpleasant and who was spitting blood about any place, from the cut on his lip. The sound of it, and of Mrs. Willett's rough breathing, was stopped by the closing door.

"What a mess," Jess said. He went over to where Linda was sitting, sheet white, in a chair. "Glad you married me, Linda?" She looked at him. "I'll be going in the morning, Jess."

Jess stood very still, and his face got as white as hers. "All right," he said.

CHAPTER 7

Dr. Roger Ferris, whose job as a deputy coroner was almost entirely incidental to a general medical practice, straightened up. He sluiced a small pellet of metal in water and dropped it into a saucer on the table top. He washed his hands in a basin, dried them, and said to Valcour: "That is the bullet."

Valcour picked it from the saucer and turned it in his fingers. "A twenty-two caliber, wouldn't you say? Rifle?"

Dr. Ferris's kindly eyes were dark gray. His hair was gray. His normally ruddy cheeks were a little gray, too. "I am not very familiar with firearms, Mr. Valcour. Our infrequent deaths up here—those to which I am called in my capacity as a deputy coroner—are mostly accidental— motor accidents, unfortunate drownings, hunting deaths in which there has never been any question as to the weapon." He stared intently down upon Arthur's body. "There is something singularly pitiful about this."

They were alone in the room. The log on the hearth no longer flamed. The embers were bright cherries, massed, shining clear, breathing.

"Let us sit down for a moment, Doctor." They drew two chairs up close to the hearth. The room was growing cold, and the embers' warmth felt good. Dr. Ferris refused a cigarette. "How long have you known the Willetts?" Valcour said.

"I've known them since the time they built this camp. That would be fifteen or twenty years, about." Dr. Ferris's kind, elderly face broke into the smile that came so easily to it. "Time seems to go faster nowadays than it did when I was young. It is difficult to keep accurate track."

"Life has speeded up on us, Doctor."

"I think we have lost the art of leisure. I remember, sir, when…"

Valcour waited patiently until he was through. It seemed to him as though Dr. Ferris were almost doing it deliberately: steering so sharply clear of their main and important course. Valcour took the first break as an opportunity to say: "Do the Willetts use this camp much?"

"They did when Allenby Willett was alive. There, Mr. Valcour, was a curiously strange man—difficult, very difficult, I should imagine, to live with. I used to think of springs when I would be with him. Coiled springs, soft, and continually bouncing. Kate—" He paused and shrugged. Then he said: "Of course, she loved him. It was most unfortunate, and distinctly against my advice. He would consult me. I was frequently here as a guest."

"What was, Doctor?"

"Sir?"

"Unfortunate?"

"Why, Henry and Arthur. Absurd of a man of his age and general condition to want children. He had Jess. It wasn't as if they were childless. But he was not a man who would listen easily to reason. Springs, soft coiled springs. I am not suggesting, Mr. Valcour, that Allenby Willett was insane. He was no more insane than you or me, than any man, shall we say, of professional intelligence."

Valcour laughed and said: "You classify ourselves, professional men, as slightly so?"

"Certainly. The zero level of sanity is, to my way of thinking, complete and conventional dumbness. Sheep are sane, both animal and human. Let us take for example an average man of the laboring classes…"

He was off again, and Valcour smoked and listened to a lengthy and not uninteresting discourse on the well springs of human behavior. He said, at its conclusion: "From your intimate knowledge of the Willett family, can you suggest any further motives, than the obvious one, for this crime?"

Dr. Ferris looked genuinely surprised. "Motives? I understood Kate to say there had been notes, threatening notes."

"There have been. They stick out in this case like a bright metal signpost." Valcour smiled and added, "I don't want to get hypnotized by concentrating on them exclusively."

"I do not believe that I quite understand."

Valcour sheered off. "Do you agree with me, from my description as to where Arthur was sitting when shot, that the gun was fired from the vicinity of the dining-room doorway?"

"Unquestionably, sir. I do not quite see how you failed to notice the sound."

"A log on the hearth was blazing at the time—sharp pops—loudly—the sound from a twenty-two would not have been noticeably identifiable above it."

Dr. Ferris refused to be put off. "To get back to those notes. Mr. Valcour. I do not see how there can be any argument as to their not being the sole and definite motivation for this crime."

"Does it not occur to you, Doctor, that they could have been written by someone as a blind, as a false lead toward a fictitious outside agency?"

"Those are just theories, Mr. Valcour?" Dr. Ferris felt miserably shocked.

"Let us rather call them possibilities. And all possibilities must be examined."

There was a delicate hesitation. "Do you intend advancing them at the inquest?"

Valcour returned Dr. Ferris's troubled stare steadily. "Would you wish me to suppress them, Doctor?"

"I think you know, Mr. Valcour, that I would not wish you to suppress anything at the inquest." His face looked very drawn and old.

"And I promise you that I shall not advance any theories that are not pretty well grounded on fact. I understand that you have released the body?"

"Yes. Jess has arranged by telephone for our undertaker down at the Forks to fix things up. He will be out here in the morning. We will hold the inquest around noon, and I presume that the body will be shipped south to Woodlawn on the following day."

"Do you intend performing an autopsy?"

"Why, no, sir. Why should we? We have determined the cause of death. We have the bullet. I don't think that Kate could stand the thought of an autopsy. Those things are bad for the mind. They linger."

Valcour smiled. It was a singular business, all the way through. This man sitting beside him wasn't a coroner, he was a friend of the family. He wondered what the attitude of the sheriff would be—of the state's attorney—of the coroner's jury—of the press—of (his thoughts slowed up a little) himself. And then he noticed young Wilbur Strange standing with pale wide lips just inside the room by the hall doorway.

"Henry's pretty bad, Doctor," Wilbur said.

"Bad?" Dr. Ferris was startled by Wilbur's voice.

"He's sort of hysterical."

"We have heard nothing."

Valcour noted that Wilbur hadn't once looked toward the couch, with its burden of Arthur's neat, stiff body.

"It isn't that sort of hysterics, Doctor. It's twitches. I thought you might do something."

"Twitches?" Dr. Ferris was on his feet and reaching for his bag. "Nervous reaction—shock—nothing to worry about in the least. Twitches, you say?"

Wilbur followed after him. His face was desperately pale. He looked, to Valcour, as if he were going to be sick. "Yes, Doctor. He's twitching all over."

CHAPTER 8

Valcour did not follow them down the hallway.

He stopped at the door to the room used by Linda and Jess.

He rapped, and accepted a muffled word from inside as an invitation to come in.

"Where is he now?" he said.

Linda (even the fur coat she was wearing over her padded dressing gown could not warm the coldness) was aware of the question's curious implications, the question which had been put so gently by this man who was himself so gentle, so dangerously gentle and assured.

"I have been waiting for him," she said.

"When did Mr. Willett leave here?"

"He hasn't been here, Mr. Valcour."

"Not at all?"

"Not since he dressed for dinner."

There could be no accurate gauge for veracity in her present condition. Valcour could see that she was uncomfortably close to hysteria. "Would you mind telling me what brought you into the living room?" he said.

"Jess. I was looking for Jess. It was longer than ten minutes, you see."

He didn't sec at all, but he said: "Of course. He was going to come back to you in ten minutes, and then he didn't come."

"That's it, Mr. Valcour. He didn't come." There was a lot of parrot in the way she said it.

"Wasn't that a little contradictory? He couldn't have left you, could he, if he hadn't been in here since before dinner?"

She said: "He wasn't inside then. He couldn't get inside then."

"No?"

She knew she was saying all sorts of things, and that she shouldn't. "He spoke to me through the door. There's a bolt on the door. I had it bolted."

"And he said he would be back in ten minutes?"

"Yes, Mr. Valcour. Ten minutes." The utter meaninglessness of words. You could use a thousand of them and still not adequately explain a thing.

"It was after the ten minutes were up that you went to look for him?"

"Quite a little after. I thought he might be sitting up by the fire, but there wasn't anybody by the fire but dead Arthur."

"You passed nobody in the hall?

"No, Mr. Valcour, just dead Arthur on the couch and nobody anywhere at all."

"Thank you."

He was gone, and the door was shut. The inside of her mouth was dry. She wanted to call that man back. She had to tell him something. But the inside of her mouth was dry and her tongue was sticking to it…

Slade was in the hall by Mrs. Willett's door, just closing it, as Valcour reached it.

"How is she?" Valcour said.

"She wanted some water to take some veronal in, sir." Slade was unstrung. His thinnish, fine-featured face was paste-colored in the hall's uncertain light.

"You look pretty shot yourself," Valcour said.

"It has been a bit of a blow, Mr. Valcour."

They moved a few steps down the hall. Their voices were instinctively low. "What do you know about it?"

"Nothing, sir."

"You were fond of Arthur Willett?"

Slade raised his eyebrows nervously. "One couldn't very well be that, sir. One feels the blow for the family."

"You've been in service with them for a while?"

"Ten years, Mr. Valcour."

He said thoughtfully, "You are sure there's nothing you want to tell me, Slade?"

Slade lightly moistened his lips with the tip of his tongue. "Nothing, sir."

Valcour shrugged. "You will let me know, please, when you change your mind."

He left Slade, standing in puzzled stillness, and went on down the hall. Light came from the boys' room and Dr. Ferris, preparing a hypodermic, assured him as he looked in that his diagnosis About Henry's twitches had been correct. "Nerves, Mr. Valcour, nothing but nerves." Valcour continued to the end of the hallway and went outside onto the veranda. The cold of the windless night was a physical shock, and his flashlight was brilliant on oak flooring. Against the building's south side was a deep couch. The light from his torch stayed motionless on the rug-bundled figure lying there. Jess stirred uneasily under the light's glare, his eyes opened, he sat upright.

"What—well?" Jess said.

"Sorry to have disturbed you, Mr. Willett."

Jess threw of! blankets and sat on the edge of the couch. "I've been asleep. Cold, isn't it?"

Valcour said casually: "Why are you out here?"

Jess's laugh was not pleasant. "I prefer it." He stared out hard into the night's darkness, then he said: "How's Mother?"

"I understand that she has taken some veronal, to make her sleep."

"She was crazy about that kid."

He did not, Valcour noticed, ask for Linda.

"By the way, Mr. Willett, where were you when this happened?"

"Here."

"Here on this couch?"

"Yes. Right here."

"Sleeping?"

"No, not sleeping, Mr. Valcour. Thinking."

"Were you lying down or sitting up?"

"Lying down. Why?"

"Which end was your head at?"

"This end. Why?"

"I was wondering whether you could have seen the door that opens from the kitchen onto this veranda. I realize that you couldn't."

"That's right—that's the door—"

"It is one of the possible doors for the murderer to have taken."

Jess said sharply: "It is the only door he could have taken."

"Not necessarily, Mr. Willett. He could have gone through the kitchen door that opens into the hallway, along the hallway, and out onto the veranda by the back door."

"But why should he?"

"I don't know. And if he did, then your wife must have just missed seeing him."

"Linda? How?"

"Because she came out of her room and walked along the hall to the living room between the time that Arthur was shot and when I reached the hall door from the kitchen. I was about three minutes or less in reaching that door. Wilbur Strange must have just missed him, too. Mr. Strange had also passed along that hallway before I had reached its kitchen door."

"It is queer," Jess said thoughtfully, "that Linda or Wilbur or I saw nothing."

"Quite queer. Of course the position you were in on the couch would have prevented you from seeing the veranda door, but did you hear anything? The sound of anyone moving off? Running?"

"Not a thing."

"The pine needles would deaden near-by footsteps, but out in the underbrush?"

"If I did hear anything, I didn't notice it."

"Let us go on from your lying here, Mr. Willett."

"Go on?"

"Yes. You were lying here on the couch about the time the shot was fired. Then you were coming through the dining-room doorway into the living room. That is when we first saw you, if you remember. How did you get there?"

"Through the kitchen—through the pantry—through the dining room. Why?"

"That's it," Valcour said softly. "Why?"

"Why?"

"Yes. What made you get up from the couch and come in just then. Anything?"

"How in hell do I know, Mr. Valcour?"

"Coincidence, then?"

"I didn't 'feel' anything, if that's what you mean. I didn't hear anything. I just got up and went. People do just get up and go, don't they?"

Valcour said pleasantly: "Indeed they do."

Jess stood up. "Is Dr. Ferris through with Arthur?"

"Quite through."

"Then I'll go in."

Jess was gone, and the snap of a twig in the blackness beyond the veranda's rim sounded loudly. Valcour stood motionless and aimed his flashlight toward the snapping. He pressed the button. "I see you have it," he said quietly.

Larry kept on walking toward him, along the lane cut by the torch's bright white light. Larry had a small gun in his hand, a twenty-two caliber target rifle. Larry stopped beside Valcour on the veranda and handed him the gun. "I guess it's it, all right."

Valcour took a handkerchief from his pocket and wrapped it about the gun's barrel. He held it by the handkerchief and sniffed the muzzle.

"Where did you find this gun, Mr. Stone?"

"I stumbled against it just now, coming along the path."

"Near the veranda?"

"Well, the path's about twenty feet from the veranda."

"Then it wasn't this path right here?"

"No, Mr. Valcour. It was the one that runs along the other side of the house. It cuts off in the direction of the garage."

"What were you doing, Mr. Stone?"

"Doing? Just looking around. I felt that somebody should. The Moore boys were so little help that I thought maybe I could do something. I did. I got that gun."

"Do you recognize it?"

"Well, it's a common type, Mr. Valcour. It might be one of ours, as the place is packed with guns. It's been fired pretty recently."

Valcour studied Larry's face, dimly pale in the darkness, with tired and worried lines aging its youngness. "That path on which you found this gun, Mr. Stone, it runs, doesn't it, past the bedroom windows?"

Larry didn't say anything for a moment. Then he repeated almost stupidly, "Yes, past the bedroom windows."

CHAPTER 9

The night was a dreary waste of endless hours, and Valcour passed the bulk of it with Dr. Ferris, in chairs drawn close to the living-room hearth. Arthur's body had been taken from the couch and placed on a lounge in the gun room, where it lay in that peculiar immobility which is so in harmony with the incomprehensible qualities of night. And Wilbur Strange was sitting wide-eyed and fully dressed where he could watch it, gripped in its special stillness, this curious sculpture, so devastatingly motionless in its waxed mask.

Larry was lying on a couch in the room with Henry, and Mrs. Willett, with her veronal, slept on. Linda was not in her room, and neither was Jess, but Valcour wasn't worried about them.

He had made a silent, final tour: first to the garage, where he had fixed the timers on the cars so that they could not start, and then for a brief circling of the near-by paths, needle thick and soft with pine, scratches in vastness, in stillness, as if the night slept too. He had stood for quite a while at the spot where Larry had found the gun, looking thoughtfully across the bare twenty-foot stretch of pine needles to the house, to its veranda…and to its windows…

He had stopped short on his tour of the veranda, stopped very close to the deep, broad couch on its southern end, because of the crying; not especially noisy, but thick, and endless, and unhappy crying. He had stared at the two of them, bundled beneath rugs—at Jess and Linda—at Jess, who was in her arms—at Jess, who was crying. He had turned and retraced his steps and had gone inside—wondering—thinking…

Using his flashlight, Valcour had made a deliberate and minute search in the kitchen, pantry, dining room, and hallway for clues. Clues were, he reflected, staring down at a bit of suet that had evidently missed the garbage pail by the kitchen sink, unfortunately rarely labeled. Blood, fingerprints, footprints, daggers, guns—their obviousness made them doubly welcome. But the commonplace things, things which fitted so blendingly into every-day living (that piece of suet might well be a case in point) that one ignored them, and yet which might fit so vitally into the jigsaw of a puzzling problem—they were the dues that were never labeled. He resisted a strong temptation to gather in the suet. If he ever, he told himself, started that…

Dr. Ferris was in a chair by the living-room fire. He wanted to know the time.

"It is three o'clock, Doctor."

"Thank you. The most comfortable chair is a wretched thing to sit in for the night. I am getting old, Mr. Valcour."

Valcour got a log from the container and placed it on the fire. He sat down in a chair near the doctor's. "I don't see why you won't lie down on the couch. There is no need for both of us to stay awake."

Dr. Ferris's weary eyes stared at the flames from beneath lowered lids. "You have disturbed me. You have me thinking things, feeling things. I do not like it." His voice was momentarily angry. "My dear man, what motive can there be beyond those notes?"

Valcour was gravely serious. "When we find it, I believe that it will be unique." He said nothing for a troubled moment. "I have the feeling that there are forces operating in this case that I dislike to interfere with."

"Why do you say that?"

"Because I think that there are in life certain elementary—what can we call them? Values? Reasonings? Intuitive strengths?—that are so powerful that they had best be left alone. We cannot divert them, our laws cannot divert them, any less futilely than that feeble gesture made by Canute in defiance of the sea."

"It is strange to hear you talk like this, Mr. Valcour. Such matters rightly belong to my profession rather than to yours."

"I must disagree. For the detection of ordinary crime, yes. But for the obscure, the extraordinary—well, a certain deeper insight into human behavior is an essential of greater importance than any talent for the observing and deducing of clues."

"Aren't you reading a great deal into what is really a simple and straightforward case, Mr. Valcour?"

"Doctor, I am not. I wish that I were. I wish that I could convince myself of its simplicity."

Dr. Ferris said suddenly: "Is it your intention to make an arrest?"

"Good heavens, no. Have you the slightest idea of the amount of evidence necessary for making out a prima-facie case against a person for the purpose of indictment? It's tremendous. Remember that no witness actually saw the shooting, and that in order to bring guilt home it will be necessary for us to get sufficient circumstantial evidence—if you will permit me to be legally wordy—to destroy the presumption of innocence and to remove what otherwise might be reasonable doubt of guilt. Unless this is competently and carefully done, Doctor, any clever defense attorney can move and generally get the dismissal of an indictment. And what have we here? There isn't enough circumstantial evidence lying around loose to trouble the eye of a mote. Premature arrests are singularly comparable to premature explosions, in that they generally do the major damage to the person who has instigated them."

"Then the inquest, Mr. Valcour?"

"I think it will commendably result in a verdict of murder by person or persons unknown."

Dr. Ferris said slowly, "And after the inquest?"

Valcour shrugged. "If the state's attorney or the sheriff pleases, we will continue to accumulate facts. Should enough of them be found, they will be presented to the Grand Jury, who will then indict or not. If they do bring in a true bill, the case will come up in the trial court, after the customary several months' delay."

"It's a lengthy business."

"That is sometimes according to how much oil there is poured on justice's reputed wheels."

Their voices died in the night's deep hush, and the doctor's head sank lower upon his chest, and after a while Valcour said to him: "What are you thinking about?"

"Of Kate Willett. This shock to her. It will be months before she actively begins to feel it. I hope that someone competent is with her when she does. The nervous system, Mr. Valcour, is a damnably strange thing."

Minutes drifted slowly into minutes and there was no sound in the building or in all the surrounding night. Window panes paled greyly and the log on the hearth was ash. Chill of morning was seeping—seeping.

"You are worried about something," Dr. Ferris said.

"I am worried," Valcour said quietly, "about the murder which we may yet have to prevent."

Dr. Ferris stared sharply. "You think that this scoundrel will next get after Henry?"

"Disassociate your mind for a moment from the extortion idea. Think of their hair. Think of the backs of their heads."

"Whose, sir?"

"Of Arthur—of Henry—of Jess."

"Similar, yes. Quite similar. My dear Mr. Valcour! The hair and the back of the head—that was all that the murderer could have seen when Arthur was shot."

"That's the point, Doctor. You see, Jess Willett was sitting on the same spot on that lounge not more than two minutes before the shot was fired."

CHAPTER 10

Mrs. Willett did, to Valcour's intense astonishment, appear for breakfast. The lids of her overlarge eyes were red, her nose was red, and the mottles on her face were more pronounced, standing brown upon a dead white skin. Her dress was a shirt-waisted black broadcloth arrangement that went a good way to proving the theory of reincarnation. She insisted upon eggs. In an effort to pin her shattering mind on normalcy, she clung to a determination that everyone must have and eat some eggs. "So strengthening." She tried, with this, to clinch Linda, whose own eyes were weary and lusterless flowers placed in beauty. "Try, dear child— just one. We have an energetic day before us. The inquest will be held at noon, I believe you said, Doctor?"

Dr. Ferris looked at her searchingly and said: "Yes, Kate."

"Then lunch will be indefinite. I don't know how long such things last—?" She appealed to Valcour.

"I should say in this instance not more than two hours, Mrs. Willett." He was astonished at her control—with Arthur dead, with Henry deep in exhausted sleep.

"So foolish of Wilbur not to come in," she was saying. "Proper sustenance is essential. He insists upon staying in there with Arthur. So foolish—so kind." Wetness splashed sharply down her cheeks, and Larry said quickly: "How about eating an egg yourself, Kate? You've been bamboozling the lot of us into downing them. How about yourself?"

Her eyes were drying again, and she said, "Dear Larry!" and broke the shell from the top of an egg and did things elaborately with pepper and salt. "I must remember to speak to Slade about the coffee. It's in that indeterminate stage, this morning, between itself and tea. You are a bachelor, Mr. Valcour?"

His smile was bolstering. "Yes, Mrs. Willett."

"Then such matters don't bother you. I have always imagined that a bachelor's life must be an uninterrupted succession of dishes perfectly cooked, with their origin conveniently wrapped in mystery."

"Then you imagine wrong."

"Really?"

"I could prove it to you some time, if you'll breakfast with me in my apartment. I've a man whose sole grasp on the art of cooking lies in the conviction that some food is served wet, and some dry."

"He must be a fundamentalist. Larry, another egg?"

"Good God, no, Kate. I've had two. My sense of devotion and my stomach are absolutely stabilized."

"Doctor?"

Dr. Ferris shook his head.

"Jess, dear boy—you must."

"No, thanks." Jess's voice was frayed, and his eyes were very bright, very dry, and had no littleness. He stared at no one, at nothing, his hand mechanically raised and lowered a cup of steaming coffee, which he sipped.

"Toast, dear, then?"

"No!" The word was an explosion. He took the cup in his hand and sent it crashing across the room to shatter on the facing wall. He stood up, in the utter, the overpowering stillness. He steadied himself for an instant with his hand on the back of Linda's chair. He found, and went out of, the door. Dr. Ferris stood up abruptly and went out after him.

The silver bell in Mrs. Willett's hand was sharply clear, and Slade, with discreet and troubled eyes, came in from the pantry and stood waiting.

"Some fresh toast, Slade."

"Yes, madam."

"Eggs?" Her smile was a grimace in granite, while her look brushed Larry and Valcour and Linda. "No eggs."

"Yes, madam."

Slade's glance at the broken cup was impersonal. It flickered for an instant toward the doorway through which Jess and Ferris had just gone. He left the room.

Mrs. Willett's large-knuckled fingers were fondling Linda's ice-cold hand. "Such moments are trying, my dear. They are rare. Life is a pleasant stream"—she hesitated for a moment, and during it oldness grew set in her, planted so solidly in her that she knew she could never again warm herself with the false illusion that it could be shaken away—"if you keep," she went on, "the boat you're riding in on top. That sounds like the curtain in a play—a very bad curtain in a very bad play, but at heart I'm an emotional fool."

"Would you mind?" Linda stood up.

"Not at all. But if you'll accept my advice, I'd leave him alone."

Linda's smile was a distortion. She went outside, and they could hear her footsteps running—running—running.

"I say, Kate, as soon as we can let's cut this." Larry's voice was a clear windy blast. "Shove off, I mean—France—Spain—the Islands—what do you say?"

Her face was very weary, very tired. "It would be lovely to find the sun again. If we can, dear Larry. If we can."

"What's to prevent?"

She said quite steadily: "Perhaps Mr. Valcour could tell you better than I."

"Oh?" The buoyancy was gone from Larry's voice. It was guarded.

"I hope that nothing need interfere, Mrs. Willett."

"That is good of you, Mr. Valcour."

"There will naturally be a certain period during which it may be advisable for us to keep in touch."

She stood up and went to the door. "I quite understand," she said. Her hair was sleekly silver, her face incredibly pinched, and so very tired. Her eyes stayed with them as she turned and walked away.

"Rotten business," Larry said.

"Murder is."

They were both standing, moving toward the door.

"I'm going outside where there's air," Larry said. "Coming?"

"Not just now."

Larry was at the front door. He opened it and went out onto the veranda. Valcour crossed to the telephone extension that was on a table in a corner of the living room. He put through a call to New York and hung up the receiver. The operator would ring him when the connection was made.

He took the report that he had written last night from his pocket and tore open the envelope. He removed from it the blank sheet of paper and the envelope addressed to Mrs. Willett. They would now have to be offered in evidence at the inquest. And the report to the commissioner would have to be amended. He would of course tell the commissioner all that was advisable—as much as it was advisable to tell over a public telephone, and few telephones were as devastatingly public as those operating through a country exchange.

The stillness was incredible.

Death alone could not have caused it. The building itself was clamping him in an absolute hush. He found that he was walking about as uneasily as a cat. He stopped abruptly at the door to the gun room and looked in—at Arthur's sheeted body—at Mrs. Willett and Wilbur Strange, locked tightly, standing, her tired tight blackness crushed to him and her cheeks slow-soundless rivers while his eyes, as they stared back at Valcour were of ice blackly surfacing profound and dangerous depths.

CHAPTER 11

The inquest, which was held in the living room of the camp building, resulted as Valcour had predicted with the customary verdict. There had been several features in it that had startled him. It had been a distinct shock that Slade's testimony should have been so sensational, and Mrs. Willett had interested him too. Especially when she was giving her testimony concerning the threatening notes. It amused him to see the avidity with which the coroner's jury of neighboring men seized on them and swallowed them whole. Threat notes, to their way of thinking, were inseparably connected with celebrated crime, and the important standing which the Willett family had for years held in their community unquestionably placed the crime in that class.

With Valcour's interpretation of the threat-note business in mind, Dr. Ferris had made an effort to slur it over, whether consciously or not, but the jury wouldn't have it. They were, the notes, such a clear and tangible motive, perfectly reasonable, and perfectly plain. Mrs. Willett stood in their eyes as an extremely rich woman (which she was) and as a figure in cosmopolitan society (which she had, during the earlier years of her marriage, certainly been) and they believed that women of her type were frequently the prey of extortionists. They flatly refused Dr. Ferris's rather clumsy slurring. They wanted details—explicit, complete.

The jury's foreman, Fred Salters (he owned one of the garages down at the Forks and his evenings were divided into two parts, the first of which was devoted to emphatic if somewhat novel contract bridge, and the second to journals of crime), wanted to know just exactly why Mrs. Willett had destroyed the notes.

"I don't quite understand, Mrs. Willett, why you didn't keep them."

"I have already explained, Fred"—she had known him back in his gawky youth—"that there were instructions in the notes to destroy them as soon as I had read them. Also, I didn't want the boys to see them."

"I know, but couldn't you have hidden them some place?"

"I'm not very good at hiding things. And you know how the boys are—" For one stabbing second she caught her breath sharply at the inaccurately inclusive tense and then went on, leaving it unchanged, as

Arthur's presence in her heart would always be unchanged, always living—never, never… "They're into everything. Everything."

Dr. Ferris stared at the jurymen, vaguely troubled. "I don't see, gentlemen, the advantage in rehashing this line of inquiry. Mrs. Willett has already stated that she destroyed the notes, and why."

"I know it, Doc," Fred Salters said, "but it seems such a shame. Can't you even remember what was in them, Mrs. Willett?"

"Why, yes, in a general way. The first one came last August. I do not remember the date, except that it was in the early part of the month. We were then at Southampton, in a cottage we had rented—Larry, Wilbur, and the boys and I. Jess was with Linda's people, visiting them in Maine. The letter—the first note—came in the morning mail. It was on the table with the rest of my mail when I came down to breakfast." (It was this circling that interested Valcour, this slow and needless swinging around the essential point, this deliberate shielding of something, or someone—but the jury were pleased with it, and hugged each word.) "There was nothing peculiar about the envelope, nothing indicative, I mean, of the nature of the message inside. White, I'm sure the envelope was, and of good quality linen. I remember it was postmarked in New York City. All of the envelopes were postmarked in New York City."

"What did it say, Mrs. Willett?"

"I believe that first message read: you love your three sons—you are a woman of wealth—you must share some of that wealth with me, or your two younger sons will be kidnapped or worse."

"Golly! How many more notes were there, Mrs. Willett?"

"Two—rather, three. The second came while we were stopping at the Plaza. We don't bother very much with opening the town house." She indulged in one of her rare smiles. "It's rather an enormous thing and always gives me the feeling that it isn't a house, so much, that I'm opening as a parliament." Fred Salters grinned pleasantly. He had always liked Mrs. Willett. There had never been anything stuck up about her. He found himself liking her even better. "What was in that second note?" he asked.

"It was more definite. It mentioned the sum of twenty thousand dollars, and was explicit about my not taking the matter up with the police."

"You didn't pay it, did you?"

"How could I? Nothing was said as to where the money was to go, or to whom. It just stated that I was to have the money on hand in cash. Well, I did."

"You got that money in cash?"

"In hundred-dollar bills. I have it now."

Valcour stared at her sharply. She had said nothing about this, about having the money actually in her possession. She had been upset, of course—miserably upset—but still… She felt his look and returned it steadily, almost impersonally, then she turned again to Fred Salters.

"You got the money here now in this camp?" he was saying.

"Yes."

"Then you were going to pay it over?"

"I was."

"Why didn't you?"

"Because the man was not there to receive it."

"How is that, Mrs. Willett?"

"The third message came over a week ago. We were still at the Plaza, planning a trip. One of those round-the-world things, you know, where they even arrange the sunrise. I had thought it best to go away for a year or two after this business was settled. That third note said to take the money in a small over-night bag and walk west from the northwest corner of Fifth Avenue and Forty-second Street to Times Square. I was to start exactly at noon. I don't know whether you know how crowded the street is at that hour. Walking becomes a question of the vertical, rather than the horizontal."

"I'll say I do, Mrs. Willett. I wouldn't live in that town for the world. It's all right to visit, but to live there—no sir. I'd suffocate. I'd feel all cramped in."

She let him get the favorite, nation-wide dictum off his chest, and then went on: "According to the note, someone would come up beside me during those two blocks and press my arm three times. I was to give him the bag. The idea was quite clever. No one could be traced or followed through that crowd. Well, I walked the two blocks. Nothing happened."

They were obviously disappointed. "Nothing?" Fred Salters said.

"No."

"Did you do it again—the other way?"

"Walk back towards Fifth? Yes. And then back again to Broadway. I took a taxi and returned to the Plaza."

"But didn't they get in touch with you again, Mrs. Willett?"

"Not then. I waited for several days. It wasn't very pleasant. I went down to see the commissioner."

"The police commissioner?"

"Yes. We knew each other rather well when we were both younger. I believe that I almost made the art of dancing palatable for him at Dodsworth's. There was something about a villainous set of cerise-colored ribbons that I wore, and twelve-button white kid shoes—" She brought herself up reluctantly from this irrepressible plunge into that happiness. Into that past. "He was extremely kind. He permitted Lieutenant Valcour to come up here with us until this business should have been settled." Her voice was a little thick, but quite steady, as she added: "As it has been."

"You said, Mrs. Willett, that they didn't try to get in touch with you 'then.' Did they later?"

"Yes. Up here."

"Here?"

"Yesterday, in the afternoon mail. There was another letter. It just had a word printed on it: 'Soon.'" Her voice was getting dreadfully thick, and she wanted to ask for a glass of water. "The ink must have been chemically treated, because the word had disappeared when I showed the paper to Mr. Valcour."

"Was that destroyed, too?"

"No. I believe that Mr. Valcour still has both it and its envelope."

Valcour said to Dr. Ferris: "Would you like to have them offered in evidence?"

"If you please."

"Should we touch them?" Fred Salters said, when Dr. Ferris had handed the envelope and the blank sheet of paper over for the jury to examine. "Fingerprints, I mean?"

Valcour said: "It will do no harm to touch them. But with the coroner's permission, I would like them back again."

The blankness of the sheet fascinated them more than the other two exhibits had—the bullet, and the gun, carefully wrapped in cloth to preserve its surface for the experts who would examine it later—and they enjoyed it for a full five minutes before passing it back to Valcour, who returned it to his pocket.

Dr. Ferris said, "If no one has anything further to say touching upon this line of the inquiry, we will let it drop."

"I beg your pardon, sir, but I have."

They stared at Slade, quietly standing, with his negative discreet eyes almost hidden under lowered lids.

"Well?"

"I drove into the village with one of the Moore boys for supplies yesterday. I got all the afternoon mail from the post office, sir. There was no letter in it for Mrs. Willett."

CHAPTER 12

Valcour watched light rouging on Mrs. Willett's cheeks grow prominent as blood drained from the skin beneath. She said: "Then it was placed in the mail between the time that you left the letters on the hall table, and when I looked through them."

"Yes, madam." Slade's face was miserably bleak. "If Dr. Ferris will permit me to say so, I was not presuming to bring up any doubt as to the letter having actually been received. It just occurred to me that the point might be of importance, might help"—he floundered a little, and his hands made an ineffective gesture of futility—"in clearing up this unhappy—this unhappy thing—the fact that the message did not come through the mail, but was placed among the letters on the hall table after I had brought them back from the post office."

"Of course it's of importance," Fred Salters said.

Dr. Ferris interrupted sharply. "It is of importance if Slade was not mistaken."

"I doubt whether I could have been, sir."

"Why?"

"I went through the letters twice. I always do, sir. Sometimes wrong mail is placed in our box by mistake."

Dr. Ferris stared at him heavily. "How many letters were there yesterday?"

"About a dozen, sir. Mr. Willett received most of them." He cleared his throat nervously, and then added, "Several were for Mr. Strange."

(Has he, Valcour wondered, got his knife out for young Strange? What was it he was edging around and yet not touching? He couldn't know anything vitally definite, or he would speak about it. Valcour knew Slade's type: no coercion would prevent the man from giving testimony in the cause of justice, even if that testimony had to be given against his own flesh and blood. It was planted all over his face.)

"Was there any letter for Mr. Larry Stone?" Dr. Ferris was asking.

Slade thought about this, "I don't believe so, sir."

"Aren't you sure?"

"No, sir."

"Then how can you be sure that there wasn't one for Mrs. Willett?"

Slade's colorless cheeks were reddening. "Because it was unusual. Mrs. Willett generally receives several letters in a mail."

But there was a vague, a noticeable doubt created of Slade's credibility, rather of his infallibility, and the jury's pursuit of this new line was desultory.

Fred Salters did ask: "What time was it when you put those letters on the hall table?"

"I don't know, sir. Around four o'clock, or four-thirty, I should judge."

"About when did you look through them, Mrs. Willett?" She was very decisive. "Shortly before six. I went into my room as soon as I found the letter. I read it." Her smile was there again—brief—unpracticed. "After I had read it, I automatically followed one of those customs of a lifetime, and dressed for dinner."

"Then it must have been between four, or four-thirty, and six that that letter was slid in with the others."

With this masterly bit of deduction the matter closed. Linda, Jess, Larry, Wilbur Strange—their stories were clear, unimportant, perfunctory, and accepted without quibble. Dr. Ferris himself explained Henry's nervous physical condition as the cause for his inability to testify personally—last night's severe mental shock, the boy's present exhaustive sleep—and Mr. Strange had ably stated that Henry had been constantly with him and could not, therefore, have had any personal knowledge that would be of value in solving the crime which had resulted, so tragically, in his brother's death.

The Moore boys, dazzlingly shaved and polished, were ruggedly honest, dependable, and dull. They had patrolled. Beyond a scatter of astonished and insulted wild life, they had seen nothing. They had heard nothing, until the five shots fired into the air by Mr. Valcour had temporarily separated them from their skins, and they had come a-running.

Everyone felt when he took the stand, as the last witness to be called, that whatever bombs Slade might have up his sleeve had already been exploded.

"Where were you born, please?" Dr. Ferris attacked his private notion of what was appropriate for the preliminaries in questioning any witness at an inquest, and prepared to rattle Slade's testimony right through.

"In England, sir. London."

"Are you now a citizen of the United States?"

"Yes, sir. I am naturalized."

"What is your occupation in this household?"

"Butler."

"How long have you been in service with the family?"

"Over ten years, sir."

"Will you tell these gentlemen, please, what you know of last night?"

(There is something, Valcour decided, carefully studying Slade's pale damp face, on the tip of that man's tongue.)

"I'm afraid that I don't know very much of anything, sir. About last night." The pause, the faint emphasis, were distinctly apparent.

"Where were you when the shooting occurred?"

"In my room, sir."

"In bed?"

The hesitation was there again. "Not in bed, sir."

"What were you doing?"

"I was preparing for bed, sir."

"Hear anything in the kitchen? Your room adjoins the kitchen, doesn't it?"

"Yes. I heard nothing in the kitchen." Moist beads on his forehead were more prominent. "I went to sleep early, sir. I should judge about ten."

"How were you made aware of this tragedy?"

"Mr. Valcour called me. I again dressed hurriedly and went with him into the living room."

Dr. Ferris asked perfunctorily, as he had asked each of the other witnesses, "Do you recognize this gun?"

(Can this be it? Valcour asked himself. Slade's cheeks were putty.)

"Yes, sir."

Dr. Ferris said sharply: "It is one of the guns belonging to this camp?"

"I couldn't swear as to that, sir—I am under oath, am I not?" Slade was wretchedly nervous and distressed.

"Certainly you're under oath. I asked you if you could identify this gun."

The jurymen were very quiet, and Valcour could sense the psychological tension spreading through them.

"I saw it yesterday morning, that gun, or a gun that was very much like it, in her hand."

"In *her* hand?"

Tension gripped them in its vise, making their eyes follow Slade's miserable and unhappy eyes, to where Linda was sitting beside Jess, dreadfully beautiful, dreadfully pale, and very still. "Yes." And Slade bowed toward Linda, once.

They did not want this. They did not want it at all, and Dr. Ferris finally forced himself to say: "Well, there's nothing so unusual or remarkable in that, I'm sure."

"No, sir. Not in that."

"A perfectly natural thing. Have you anything further to add to it?"

"What was said, sir."

"By Mrs. Jess Willett?"

"Yes."

"Well?"

"She said the bullet was too small to hurt, and that the sound was too gentle to hear. She was upset. I did not understand why she should say such things, sir. I did not understand why she should say such things to me."

The room was abominably quiet, and Slade's low, nervous voice lingered on in the deep stillness—dispassionately—insistently.

"This was yesterday morning, you say?"

"Yes, sir."

"At what time?"

"After breakfast."

"What time was that, please?"

"About ten o'clock, sir."

"Did you see the gun at any later moment during the day?"

"No, sir. I haven't seen the gun again until now."

Dr. Ferris said deliberately: "That is all you can tell us?"

"All, sir."

"Thank you." Dr. Ferris watched Slade walk with curious dejection back to the chair he had occupied in the rear of the room. "Would it bother you very much," he said to Linda, "if we were to recall you to the stand and ask you a few more questions?"

CHAPTER 13

It was at her again, that iciness, that uncontrollable faint trembling of her lower lip, and even the quick strong pressure of Jess's hand as she stood up didn't help it any. "Why, not at all, Dr. Ferris," Linda said, and found that her voice was reassuringly intelligible. She sat down on the witness chair, and her smile was fixed glass.

There is satisfaction in genuine beauty, and the men on the coroner's jury found it in Linda. They liked looking at her. There were no hardened or sophisticated edges to her, nor any loose softnesses. Just right, Fred Salters felt, everything about her—a lovely, splendid, clear fresh apple (his leanings were rather toward the fruit than the floral kingdom)—not a real apple smell, of course—her French perfume at twenty-four dollars an ounce was a releaser of the imagination rather than any definite scent—it conjured wine, stars, the sea, and bright blue sky—whatever one cared for most—or, to get back to Fred Salters, apples.

"Would, you care to verify Mr. Slade's testimony concerning those remarks about the gun?"

"It was quite correct, Doctor."

"The gun was one that you just happened to pick up around the camp here, wasn't it?"

"Yes." She wondered whether her smile was as painful to look at as it was to herself.

"Do you remember where you found it?"

"In a corner. I think somewhere in this room. I think that corner over there."

"You were just examining it out of curiosity?"

"Partly. I've always been familiar with guns. My home is in Maine, you know." Her smile was briefly tinged with some real warmth. "We've always been sort of a shooting family—birds—deer."

"Then naturally you would be interested." Dr. Ferris (his strewing of roses to smooth out the difficulties in Linda's path had struck Valcour as, to say the least, quaint) beamed at her pleasantly. "And after you examined the gun, you put it back again in that corner?"

"No, Doctor."

"No?"

"No"

Dr. Ferris cleared his throat. "What did you do with it?"

Her cheeks held bright and over-red spots. "I took it into my room."

He threw out another life belt. "To use it later during the day, perhaps, for some target practice?"

"If you wish."

His look at her said: really, my dear girl, if you won't play up to me… He fervently hoped that she wasn't going to slop over into hysterics; his practiced eye saw that she was dangerously near to it… "You do not understand," he said. "We are simply trying to trace the movements of this gun. Did you leave it in your room?" If she wouldn't do anything to save herself, God knows…

"Yes"

"When was that, please?"

"Just after breakfast."

"Whereabouts in your room did you leave it?"

"Standing in a corner, Doctor."

Dr. Ferris said carefully: "Did you go back to get it at any time yesterday and find it gone?"

"Well, I noticed last night when I went in to go to bed that it wasn't there."

"I see. Quite right. We will not bother you very much more, my dear. Mr. Slade has told us that you were upset; that you made a statement which he failed to understand. Had there been anything out of the ordinary to upset you?"

Her voice was forcibly steady. Her eyes were hot-looking, but quite direct. "Nothing, Doctor. We had spent the night on the train. You know that it gets in at Plattsburg uncomfortably early. I do not sleep very well on the train. If I seemed upset, it would have been due to that. I don't know why I said those things about the gun. People often say absurd and meaningless things when they're tired, don't you think?"

"Often. Thank you."

Linda stared at him. "That's all?"

"That is all."

Dr. Ferris waited until Linda had taken her seat again beside Jess. Then he proceeded to give what Valcour considered was the most barefaced summing up of a case that he had ever known. "Gentlemen, I believe that we can now reconstruct this distressing crime with a fair degree of accuracy. We can assume that the extortionist who committed this murder followed the Willett family up here. It is obvious that he concealed himself yesterday somewhere in this building. I might point out that there are plenty of hiding places in the cupboards alone, to say nothing of under the beds. I will further point out that there are no dogs in the camp to have smelled this intruder out and given his presence away. We know that at some time between four and six o'clock he must have left his place of concealment and gone into the hallway. He slipped among the other mail that was there on the table the letter which Mrs. Willett found. It is highly probable that at this time he also found and took the gun which Linda Willett had carried to her room. Gentlemen, late that night this poor and depraved wretch seized a fortuitous opportunity for shooting Arthur Willett and then he left the camp building. It will be the duty of the sheriff's office and of the state police to trace and apprehend that man. I should say that our own special interest in the matter was closed. I will now ask you gentlemen to deliberate—if you consider any deliberation on these clear and obvious facts necessary—and then to let us have your verdict. If no one has anything further to say—?"

Wilbur Strange's voice was very clear in the following pause. "Is there any use?"

"I beg your pardon, Mr. Strange?"

Wilbur's voice was heavy with suppressed feeling. "Is there any use, before this unique inquest is closed, in asking exactly why Linda took that gun into her room?"

They were standing (both Linda and Wilbur) facing each other, very close, not more than seven or eight feet apart. Her hot strained eyes were as steady as his eyes, and Valcour did not believe that he had ever heard a more complete or emphatic period mark in his life than when Linda said to Wilbur Strange, in the tense muffled stillness: "None."

CHAPTER 14

The inquest closed, with its verdict of "by person or persons unknown," at twenty minutes after three, and Mrs. Willett insisted (not that any insistence was necessary) on the jurymen staying for sandwiches and coffee. She said to Larry: "Larry, my dear boy, you will have to attend to this. Stay here with them and see that they get everything they want to eat and drink. I am through. I can stand nothing more. Tell them when they leave that I am in my room, and that I thank them."

"Right, Kate. Get some sleep if you can, old girl."

For one bitter and revealing moment her face was a tragic mask. She said: "And have to wake up again?" There were people coming toward them, toward the corner where she and Larry were standing, and she felt that the final push required to topple her right over would be the forthright expressions of sympathy which the men of this kindly, rugged mountain community would offer her in their complete, in their distressing sincerity. She smiled bewilderingly, met and went past them, and went to Valcour, who had just finished a discussion with the sheriff…

"Mr. Valcour."

"Mrs. Willett?"

"I would like to talk with you for a moment, please."

"Certainly."

She went, with her meaningless smile, into the hall and along it to her room. Valcour followed her. They went inside and she closed the door. She stood with her back to him, by a window, staring unseeingly at stark chill beauty, at the friendly melancholy grouping of pine trees rising by gentle and uneven tiers into the cool, clear mountain top… "I am going to ask you to tell me, Mr. Valcour, how we stand."

He knew exactly what she meant. He said: "I think you want me to be frank, Mrs. Willett?"

"I do. I am not a weak woman, Mr. Valcour. My life has strengthened me to shocks until their effect is now, when I meet them, nullified." Her eyes left the distant, calling mountain top. She faced him directly.

"There are no fictions so amusing to me as the reputed idleness of the idle rich, as the life that is theoretically led by a Mr. Riley, and as that bed which is composed of roses." Her voice was filled with disturbing tones as she added, "When they speak about that fabulous bed, they do not mention the attendant thorns."

Valcour smiled. "I'm afraid those illusions are indestructible, Mrs. Willett. If it weren't for them, the poor wouldn't have much to live for. They're the bunch of hay before the donkey." She said quite fiercely: "The money of this world should be happiness. There is no other sort of wealth. Reckoning in it, Mr. Valcour, I am a very poor woman."

He said carefully, "You are naturally passing through a moment of strain, or singularly unhappy distress for Arthur."

She stared at him for a full minute and then said: "Arthur? There is no distress in death. Death is just a bitter heritage that is left by their dead to the living." Then she said it again in her competent and clear voice: "How do we stand, Mr. Valcour."

There was something definitely matriarchal about her. She looked exactly what she was: the head of a family. She was their guide, the buffer between their intimate livings and a world which she had come to recognize as indifferently hard. Not hard, exactly. She wouldn't mind, Valcour decided, hardness. But when those against whom she interposed this capable buffer of herself might be amused…

"You are a sensible woman, Mrs. Willett," he said. "I will speak plainly. Will you admit to me that there is a very different interpretation that could be put upon those threatening notes than the one insisted upon by Dr. Ferris?"

The mottles were sharply brown again on her old and tired white face. "Let us sit down," she said. "Will you give me your reasons for saying that?"

He did so. He then stated that his doubts frankly verged on positive disbelief that an outsider could successfully have concealed himself in the camp building for the length of time that would have been required on the preceding day—unless this outsider had been very familiar with the building's general plan and the probable movements of its occupants. And as the building was laid out on one floor and possessed only three public rooms—the living room, the dining room, and the gun room— the probable movements of its occupants would be highly problematic indeed. There wasn't, if you looked the matter coldly in the face, a moment really when you could definitely count on privacy, on not meeting someone.

And still, if Slade's testimony about the mail were dependable, this intruder, this extortionist must have been in the camp building between four and six in the afternoon in order to slip his message to her in with the rest of the letters. And he must have either stayed in the building from then on, or returned to it later when it was presumed he shot Arthur.

He touched dispassionately upon his occasional suspicions in regard to most threatening notes, and his general disbelief in a man who could flit, as the theoretical extortionist must have flitted, about unseen in a strange and well-peopled household—almost a presupposition of invisibility. He finished by saying: "Is there anything startling to you in this viewpoint?"

She sat with her large-knuckled fingers loosely meshed on her lap. He sensed a hopelessness in her eyes—her body—a look which he felt one would see on the face of a strong and capable swimmer who had misjudged the danger of the waters that lay between him and a distant shore. He felt that her resistance had reached its lowest ebb, and that if he could get her to speak now, to give some definite leads as to...

"All right," she said.

"I beg your pardon?"

Just the fact of speaking was bringing her extraordinary recuperative powers into play again. "I see the justness of your thinking so," she said. "I asked you to be frank. I shall ask you to be franker. What conceivable purpose could any member of this household have, Mr. Valcour, in killing one of my boys?" She was that swimmer again, with another wind—not her second, surely—Valcour was certain that her whole life had been a succession of winds—and her strokes were stronger, while her eyes were set with a deeper determination than ever upon that distant shore, the nature of whose haven...

"Are you convinced that Mr. Strange is trustworthy?" he asked abruptly.

"Perfectly. He would no more have written those notes..."

"I wasn't thinking so much about the notes, Mrs. Willett. I was thinking about the twenty thousand dollars."

"That?" The implication astonished her, angered her. "That is absurd, Mr. Valcour. Absurd."

"Where do you keep it?" he said.

She went over to a dresser. She took a key from a purse lying on the dresser top. She unlocked and opened a drawer. She said: "It was in here."

Valcour joined her. He knelt and closely examined the lock of the drawer. "It was opened with a key or wire," he said. "The lock isn't forced. Did you always keep it locked?"

"Yes."

"And did you keep the key in that purse?"

"Yes."

"Where did you keep the purse, Mrs. Willett?"

"Generally right here, on this dresser."

He smiled slightly. "Who knew that you had that money with you?"

"I believe no one did. I do not recall mentioning it to anyone until just now at the inquest. This is absurd, Mr. Valcour."

"Possibly. But somebody took the money. It isn't here."

"Is it useless to suggest that the writer of the notes might have searched for it and taken it with him when he escaped last night?" Her voice was very firm, very unyielding.

He deliberately ignored this. "You asked me, Mrs. Willett, what conceivable purpose any member of this household might have had in killing one of your boys. Are you familiar at all with the histories of the better-known murder cases? Take Dr. Pommerais, for example. He poisoned his mother-in-law for her failure to offer him an apology. Take the unusual Mr. Milton Bowers who, at the age of seventy-five, murdered the two Frehers—themselves about eighty—for five hundred dollars. De Jong, whose silk hat was so familiar in the capitals of Europe, and who murdered his wives by wholesale for whatever modest sums of money they might have—the famous Landru case—Dr. Crippen. No, Mrs. Willett, the 'why' in murder is perennially strange. You cannot confine it to hate, or greed, or fear. There are subtleties." He pinned her sharply with his eyes and said, "In this case there are subtleties."

She said quite calmly, "If you wish," and looked at him with her odd and defensive eyes. Then she said, as Dr. Ferris had said on the night before, "Do you intend to make an arrest? I ask this because I can see the trend of your beliefs."

He said very quietly, "Tell me what they are."

Quite suddenly she broke down completely. "You arc obsessed, Mr. Valcour—obsessed." Her voice held the uncontrolled and excited tones of oldness; there was no force, no strength in her attack—just the remnants of a magnificent will power that was being battered toward dissolution. "You are hurting me—hurting me when I can't stand it—things you couldn't understand—" She wept freely, and her breathing was miserably unmanageable. "I've tried so hard—all my life, Mr. Valcour, I've tried so hard to do what I thought was best—it isn't too much to ask, is it?—just a little happiness during these short, these ending years——"

"Mrs. Willett!" She was completely hysterical, her hands jerking spasmodically, the thick tears dripping endlessly down her cheeks.

"It isn't as if I'd ever done anything—ever—anything bad. I've always been a good woman, Mr. Valcour—I've loved my family—I've loved my husband and my children—they came first with me, always—I've never, never been first—never in my life, Mr. Valcour, have I been first—"

He felt as if she were naked, and his own throat was a tight wet clamp. There was a knock on the door, and he said sharply: "Don't come in!"

But the door opened, and Slade was standing there and saying gently, "I beg pardon, madam, but will you receive the press?"

The word had some compelling force to her. She made no effort to conceal the wretched and wet condition of her face. For a full minute she stared at Slade. She said, "Yes."

Valcour looked at her peculiarly. "I don't think that you understand, Mrs. Willett. Slade refers to reporters from the New York papers. I will explain your condition to them, or your son can satisfy them with sufficient details—"

She stood up. Her whole body seemed flooded with a singular purpose. She forced her breathing to a semblance of regularity. "Thank you, Mr. Valcour, but I understand better than you think. Slade, be good enough to say that I will be with them in five minutes."

"Yes, madam."

"But it isn't necessary—you are in no condition—you mustn't. Mrs. Willett."

He felt as if she had taken a whip and were lashing herself with it sharply.

"On the contrary, Mr. Valcour, I must."

CHAPTER 15

It was the next murder that completely upset such conclusions as the police, up to then, had arrived at concerning these crimes. There was no forewarning of it—in the sense of leads that might have included the victim potentially. (That is not exactly true; there was one very strong lead which became singularly apparent when it was recalled by Valcour in the light of later events, but during that early moment when it had showed its head above the surface in the progress of the inquest at the camp, the case had not been far enough developed to label it with any noteworthy significance.)

This second murder did not occur until immediately after the Willetts' return from their hurried and futile trip to Bermuda—futile in the sense that Mrs. Willett herself pointed out: "Mr. Valcour, you cannot escape from either a deep worry or a deep sadness. You may leave the environment of its happening miles and untold miles behind you, but you cannot leave itself. Location means nothing, distance nothing, wherever you go it goes too, it is always with you. There is nothing more futile than the hope that physical flight will bring release." Certainly no suspicion of it was in Valcour's mind during the private conference which he held with the commissioner just before the Willetts sailed.

* * * *

Mrs. Willett stopped staring at headlines.

Her sitting room, high up in the old part of the Plaza, overlooked Central Park. Her chair was near an open window, and her eyes unseeingly drifted from the lake toward the Mall, and endlessly northward into dimness. Two tiny riders on miniature horses trotted sedately along the bridle path, and the tops of the cars on Fifth Avenue were black busy bugs.

Who was it, she wondered, selected the pictures that were hung in hotel rooms. Their utter middleness oppressed her: their balanced lack either of goodness or of badness, the very stupidity of their delicate inoffensiveness against gray paneled walls…

"MOUNTAIN MURDER BLOT ON STATE CONSTABU-
LARY—What can at best be called the gross inefficiency on the
part of the…

"WRITER OF 'DEATH NOTES' BELIEVED RESIDENT
OF NEW JERSEY—Among the customary flood of anonymous
communications which are received by the police during the
investigation of any ma]or murder case was a…"

How clever of Jess to have had them all take Larry's name—Stone—
when they had booked passage for the voyage. It would be a cloak for
them behind which, during this miserable period of notoriety, they could
hide. They required no passports for Bermuda, so it was easy to use
another name…and the pictures which the reporters had taken for the
newspapers might be anybody, the only differentiation was really one
of sex…as to features…how dizzy it made you feel to look down from
a great height, although twenty stories nowadays, when you considered
the newer buildings…

They shouldn't really have come to the Plaza where for years…one
of the obscurer hotels would have been better—there were thousands of
them, weren't there?—all along the side streets in that westward section
fringing Broadway: trucks—litter—dinginess—and lobbies of marble-
ized wood…

And the boat, the blessed, dear little boat, sailed at noon, a little
prison of release on guarding waters that led into the sun…

"STATE POLICE COMBING COUNTY—The search far
the perpetrator of the murder of Arthur Willett in…"

Had she been a fool? Her fingers were loose things of flesh and bone
on her lap. If she hadn't seen the press what would they have said? Her
eyes stared dully at heaped papers about her feet. What more (her mind
emphasized the word gently) could they have said…

"I say there, Kate, old girl." Larry came into the sitting room. He had
his coat on, and his gloves. "Time to shove off. Done the drawers and
everything? You leave more things in more places than anyone I know.
You're a careless woman, and if you weren't as rich as sin you wouldn't
have a stitch on your back."

"The maid, dear Larry, I'm sure has gone through everything. Are
the bags down?"

"Bags down—bills paid—car at the door—and the boat sails in an
hour. As better comedians than I am have said, you can take it or leave
it."

The papers were a swamp about her feet—clinging—sucking—dragging. "Henry?"

Larry helped her on with her coat. "Left at least an hour ago with Wilbur. Jess has gone on ahead, too, with Linda." The last of the newspapers lay quite flat and alone on the thick soft mulberry carpet—a little paper with overlarge black letters, WHAT SCANDAL LIES BEHIND—with overlarge black letters melting crazily at their edges, slopping, dripping—if Larry didn't stop squeezing her arm so hard, he'd hurt her—

They were, she knew, in the long, sedately lighted corridor, and then by the floor clerk's desk at the elevators, with its green glass lamp shade spitting white light blindingly on white paper, and the floor clerk was saying, "…a pleasant journey, Mrs. Willett. The weather, for this season of the year…"

Mrs. Willett wondered absently whether Larry had remembered to tip her—that motherly, discreetly painted, negative looking woman just beyond the bright white light. All floor clerks seemed to her to be motherly, discreetly painted, negative women, living their sunless lives out behind desks near elevator shafts, and watching the stupid glitter of a hotel parade…

"Down, please."

She hoped that the car would stay empty. Seventeen—fourteen—ten—eight—stop—soft clashing of metal doors, and a dowdy woman in black stuffs shuffled in. Mrs. Willett recognized the woman's mustached lip as belonging to the Marchioness of Thune…that last winter at Antibes, that final desperate foolish stab at mixing in again, when her boys and the marchioness's Jock…it was coming, of course: the inevitable recognition…that guttering voice with its definite inflections of breeding: "…and Jock contracted measles shortly after we…" (It came to her in fragments, this guttering, friendly voice, as the car slid down past the remaining floors.) "…you always were a damn fool, Kate…luck… deserve…"

The lobby was a momentary release, with its circular cushioned seat and banked flowers, with its subtle air of permanent residence, and its wretched picture-of-the-moment displayed on an easel for purchase: cows, this month, in a Paris green pasture. Who *was* the genius on the staff who raked them up? And from where? The manager who for decades had always seemed to be just starting for somewhere, but who was equally always right here in the lobby no matter when you came—of course his hand was friendly—you didn't stop at a place for years and years and years…

"They have tried, Mrs. Willett," he was saying, "but we stalled them off. They think you are settled here until the town house is opened. They know that Slade's attending to opening it and…"

He referred, she knew, to reporters, and Larry's fingers were about her arm again and he was saying, "Better hurry, Kate." They were through the slow-revolving door and out onto Fifty-ninth Street's imitation of the suburbs, and a chauffeur was there at the curb, holding open the door of a motor…

Mrs. Willett leaned deeply back against the cushions. She closed her eyes and kept them closed during the car's spasmodic rushes toward the North River. The windows were down, and she felt that she could smell the various districts as they passed through them, until at last came the unmistakable acrid stench of the waterfront. Larry held her arm as they walked upstairs to the waiting room of the pier in the West Fifties. They stood until their bags were rolled up on the luggage escalator and Larry secured a porter for them. Her eyes registered briefly the couples waiting in the room—their stiltedness struck her, the almost adamantine stiltedness of people who are making their first voyage upon the sea. Even the spatter of children had caught it. Most voyagers to Bermuda, she imagined, were people who were going to sea for the first time.

They passed through a gate and started along the vast dim-ceilinged pier, and she tried to recapture some measure of the thrill she had felt on her own first voyage so many years ago—so very, very many years ago. Jess was waiting for them at the head of the gangway which stretched between the pier and the *Hamilton*'s boat deck. He looked haggard, and Linda, who was sitting near a hatch cover on a slatted wooden bench, was listless as she stood up and walked toward them through small groups of excitedly chattering people.

"Stuff all on?" Larry said to Jess.

"Should be. I spotted the trunks behind the ropes."

"Where's Henry?"

"With Wilbur."

"On board?"

"Down in their cabin."

"O.K.?"

"O.K."

"B Deck, steward." Larry indicated their bags and gave the numbers of their cabins.

The fifteen-minute bugle was sounding and the chatter became more meaningless, more hectic—the inevitable girls in tears—the useless flowers, pinned any place, held desperately—the granite-faced woman determinedly collaring a deck steward and changing the location of her chair for the third time—the smell and slosh of the river—clattering winches and noise of passing traffic, with the harassed assistant steward shepherding at the gangway the last-minute rush… Mrs. Willett felt Larry's hand and was guided by it down a companion to the promenade deck, then aft past the smoke room, the veranda cafe, then down the B Deck companion and along a passage to their cabins. It was a large cabin, hers, and the steward was racking her bags as she came in.

"All here, madam?"

She looked at the bags. "Thank you, steward."

Rest—rest—rest—two minutes of it—one—the priceless scarcity of it astonished her.

"Anything else, madam?"

"Nothing, thank you."

The door was shut. She stared through closed ports at corrugated iron. The all-ashore gong reverberated faintly through the passage outside—the liner's whistle was a deep and compelling roar—somewhere a cable slapped water, and corrugated iron started drifting tentatively past. The knock on her door was repeated. She said, "Come in." The door opened and she stared at Valcour while everything inside of her turned into heavy lead. "Of course I should have realized," she said, "that you would come too."

CHAPTER 16

Valcour came inside. He closed the door. The vibration of the ship was more pronounced, and paneling creaked. He didn't think he had ever seen a woman age so swiftly in so brief a number of days. Mrs. Willett's solidness seemed to be gone from her, leaving lines—sags—deadly tiredness. "The commissioner thought that the trip would be good for you," he said.

His voice was the small barbed hook through the lip of the fish and they, Mrs. Willett felt (Linda and Jess and Larry and Henry and Wilbur and herself), were, collectively, the fish; there was no pain, the tension was too delicately slight for pain, and the line lay almost slack upon the waters. But one didn't keep it so. Only until the fish became quite tired—so finally and very tired—and then the reel. She sat down in a cushioned armchair, but there was no comfort in it. "Will you sit down?"

"Thank you."

"What have you done?"

"I beg your pardon, Mrs. Willett?"

"What has John—what has the commissioner done?"

"I'm sorry, but I don't quite understand."

It was hurting her a good deal to think coherently. It wasn't as if she didn't have thoughts enough—her head was filled with them. How was it, she wondered, that you achieved a blessed blankness? Not in sleep. You dreamed things when you were asleep. Dead. If you were dead… her voice fumbled on:

"That we are permitted such liberty—"

"May I confine myself to technicalities?"

"Yes." It was pleasant to be monosyllabic. "Yes."

"Then the situation is approximately this, Mrs. Willett: in regard to your son's death, the state's attorney for the county is the man who has the authority to go before the Grand Jury and say, 'I want this or that person held for the following reasons,'—complicity, as a material witness, as a principal in this crime—whatever you will. He will also offer such evidence against that person as he may have. The Grand Jury then either will or will not bring in a true bill. If they do, an arrest will be made and the person either confined in jail or released on bond—a bond, usually, which constricts the person's movements to the confines of the state." Valcour stared steadily at Mrs. Willett. "I am your bond."

"It is still confusing."

"I do not mean yours personally. I refer also to your two sons, to your elder son's wife, to your nephew Larry Stone, and to young Mr. Strange."

"You have given a monetary bond?"

"No, Mrs. Willett. The commissioner, the state's attorney, the sheriff, and myself conferred. As the case now stands it is their best belief that the death of your son was the act of some person who somehow made his way into the camp unseen, and who subsequently escaped. No logical motive shows for any other explanation. They are naturally unwilling, however, that anyone who was present at the time of the crime absent them selves either permanently or too inconveniently until the case is closed. But in view of certain things—the deep friendship which the commissioner holds for you personally, for one—it was agreed that there should be a reasonable latitude of movement permitted."

Mrs. Willett stared at globs of sunlight reflected through the port holes onto the ceiling. Competent reflections of the sun. Such as she had all her life been bathed in. Never had she stood beneath its directness, its genuine, its comforting warmth… "Then you will stay with us," she said, "until the end."

"We thought it best."

The hook tugged gently at her lip and under the twinge of it she said: "As a guard, Mr. Valcour?"

He was out of his chair and standing near her, very near her, looking directly down at her and saying: "As a friend."

The word, which held for her all the desirable qualities of what living meant on earth, crushed against her face like roses. When she was young, those years and years ago, she would be foolish and would crush her face in roses. And her face, those years and years ago, had not seemed funny in the roses. If it were a trap, she didn't care. She was too tired for anything except the soothingness of that voice and of that word. She found her fingers groping hesitantly, then anchoring themselves on tweed, on an arm of firmness, while that quiet, hypnotic voice droned on… "Tell me—tell me what you know." She couldn't see, she couldn't speak because of warm wetness that was choking her. Her forehead pressed against a hand that was not her own, and a voice that was certainly not her own, even though it came from between her strained and miserable lips, was saying, "You are a good man, Mr. Valcour. You are a good, good man."

"Trust me—tell me—"

"Nothing. There is nothing."

"I am not foolish. What is this sheltering—this shielding?"

Her eyes were little and red and wet as she looked up at him, clinging still to his rough tweed sleeve. "I can't tell you." It was a child reciting from a primer, haltingly.

"Then can you tell me this." He forced her to say: "Yes, Mr. Valcour?" before he went on. "Think of the night of the murder, Mrs. Willett, and tell me why it was you took that veronal?"

The ship was beginning to feel a slight motion from the channel, and the globs of sunlight on the ceiling were swinging gently back and forth. She said, very steadily, "I needed sleep. I was tired. I am, Mr. Valcour, a tired woman."

There was a knock on the cabin door and Valcour stood up and went over to it. "Shall I open it, Mrs. Willett?"

"Please."

A stewardess stood there. She held a large bunch of yellow roses. "Shall you have these in here, madam, or do you prefer them placed on your table in the saloon?"

Mrs. Willett stood up too. She walked quite slowly over and took a card from the envelope on the ribbon. She took the flowers from the stewardess. "I'll keep them here, thank you."

"Yes, madam."

Mrs. Willett handed the card to Valcour. He knew it as that of the Police Commissioner of New York. He read on it: "Good luck." He handed it back. "I imagine you will want to rest until dinner," he said. "I believe we are all at the same table." She smiled at him a little crazily. He followed the stewardess from the cabin and shut its door.

Mrs. Willett reached uncertainly for the bolt and turned it. She held the flowers awkwardly. She couldn't feel them. She couldn't feel with her fingers at all. Only coldness. They were slipping to the floor. She was slipping to the floor, and her tired old face was crushing on the roses.

CHAPTER 17

Valcour walked thoughtfully along the passage to his cabin. The air was stuffy in it, deadened from poor circulation; in fact deadened, he decided, from no circulation. He opened one of his suitcases and got out a book, a novel. He closed the suitcase, locked it, went out and up onto the promenade deck, where remarkably little promenading was going on. A stiff breeze was chilly beneath an overcast sky, and the *Hamilton* was beginning to roll.

He saw, over the port rail, the vanishing and unattractive spider-web reliefs of Coney Island. A handful of passengers were experimentally trying out their sea legs. He liked the general looks of them. There was little of that studied indifference, that sophisticated worldliness, which you met up with so interminably on the European crossings. They looked exactly what they were—moderately rich, happy, and unimportant people off on a trip.

He kept walking forward and turned in at the smoke-room bar. The room, with its leather-covered settees and small round tables, was deserted. A card tacked on a bulletin board stated that the bar was closed until half-past four.

Valcour sat down on a corner settee and opened the book, not with any intention of reading, but to use it as an evasion from having conversation forced on him. An opened book, he had come to learn during his travels, was a pretty fair safeguard for privacy. He wanted privacy—public privacy—where there would be a certain amount of movement around him, but never touching him directly. Under such conditions, he was best able to think.

A stout man wearing gold-rimmed glasses and a self-conscious frown came in. He stared at Valcour, stared at the emptiness of the room, found a button set in the paneling, pressed it, and sat down. Nothing happened.

…Linda's marriage to Jess. Why, Valcour wondered, was it that Linda had never met the Willett family until *after* her marriage to Jess? Mrs. Willett had known that Jess was in Maine during the latter part of the summer with Linda's family. She had stated so during the inquest.

And surely it was unnatural—had it been an elopement? Nothing had been said as to any elopement.

The stout man was beginning to breathe heavily. He snorted. He stood up and pressed the button again. He stared doubtfully at Valcour, at the opened book, at Valcour's thoughtfully lowered eyes. He sat down again. Nothing happened.

…What was the basis of Wilbur Strange's control over Henry and Arthur? Over (Valcour felt decidedly that this should be included) Mrs. Willett? That single touch of Wilbur Strange's hand on Henry's shoulder had been enough, at the climax of that peculiar game of "Going to Jerusalem," to quiet him. Would the man at headquarters to whom Valcour had detailed the job of finding out certain things wireless him the results, or would they…

The stout man cleared his throat. He ignored the clock that was set in the bulkhead, took out a large gold hunter from a waistcoat pocket, and satisfied himself as to the time. He stared fixedly at Valcour. His reddish face grew delicately purple. "Where in hell is that steward?" he said.

Valcour smiled vaguely and pointed to the printed card. The stout man stood up, walked over, and read it. He again took out the gold hunter. "Poppycock!" he said. The door slammed after him as he crossed the combing onto the deck.

…What had been the real foundation for Slade's obvious agitation both on the night of the murder and during the inquest? An odd and rare character, Slade. There was a conflict going on inside of him. Between loyalty and duty? Duty to his oath, to justice? Loyalty to whom?…

The door opened and three middle-aged women came in. They looked at the leather settees. They looked at Valcour. Whatever it was, they knew it was all wrong.

"It's—" said the first.

"Exactly, Nellie. It's the barroom."

They kept their stares battered on Valcour, while Nellie mentally compared him with her steel engraving in the spare bedroom of the Rake's Progress. The third and thinnest of the women muttered something about "postcards" and they went out again on deck.

…Had Wilbur Strange's start of surprise been natural on the night of the murder when Mrs. Willett had advanced the threat notes so emphatically as the motive for the crime? Had it really been the first moment that young Strange had been aware of them?…

Two couples came in, very young, very newly smartly dressed. They glanced at Valcour, appraised him, ignored him. They took a table with four chairs and sat down. One of the young men produced two packs of cards. They started to play contract.

…Slade?…

"Diamond."

"Heart."

"Three clubs."

"Three hearts."

"Four no trumps."

"Atta-boy, Liz."

"Double."

"Hell."

"Is that a bid, Oscar darling, or just a confession of weakness?"

"Don't call me Oscar. If God made me look like a Swede, my parents at least had the kindness to name me Freddy. It's a bid."

"'Hell'?"

"Yes—no—where are we?"

"'The Ambrose Channel Light Ship, sir,' the captain's daughter cried. And, smiling, the boy fell dead."

"When does this damn bar open? I want wine—wine—I must, dear lady, have my wine."

"Five o'clock."

"Oh, it does not. It opens at four-thirty. I've memorized that card by heart."

"And that will be in twenty minutes and thank God for that."

"Do you sweet children know that this is at one half of one cent per point, and that papa has bid four no trumps?"

"Doubled, dearie."

"Yes, sweetness."

"Shoot."

…Why did Mrs. Willett take the veronal? Why had Jess been sleeping on the veranda? Did Larry really stumble against the gun on the path as he claimed, or…

"Let's see. Four no trumps doubled, not vulnerable, the four aces in one hand, and…"

"Don't bother figuring it out, darling. Just give Oscar this diamond lavaliere and your horse-head stick pin and…"

"Care to join the pool, sir?"

Valcour looked up at the steward, who had just come into the room and was standing beside him.

"How much, steward?"

"Two dollars, sir."

Valcour put his name down for the ship's pool. "Opening soon?" he said.

"In a few minutes now."

"Bring me an Irish whiskey and plain water when you do."

"Yes, sir."

"Steward—oh, my darling steward—come here."

The steward walked over to the bridge table.

"One big fat quart of champagne, my angel."

"I don't care what you say, I want a cocktail and—"

Oscar was looking down at the score. "Cyanide for me," he said.

"You can't take it straight, dear. You have to have water…"

…Why hadn't Wilbur Strange joined the others at breakfast on that morning after the crime? Had it really been as Mrs. Willett had advanced: an unshakable determination to remain on guard by Arthur's body? Why Arthur? Arthur was dead. Whereas Henry—surely what menace had still existed would presumably…

They were honeymooners, these two, who had come in and were sitting down near Valcour. She ordered sherry, and the man a bottle of beer. "It's just too wonderful," she was saying, "to be able to sit down and order what you want without having a cop walk in on you."

"When was it you had a cop walk in on you?"

"Why, Willie Peterberg, you *know* I—"

"When was it, if you please, that that cop walked in on you?"

…Where were the twenty thousand dollars? Had there (Valcour played delicately with the thought) ever been any twenty thousand dollars?…

"It was that night at the Tomb when Archie Leverest and—"

"That sap."

"Why, Willie Peterberg, how can you say such things about…"

"Diamond."

"Heart."

"Three clubs."

"Say, what is this? A return engagement?"

"Play your cards, my good man, and no remarks from the peanut gallery."…

…"I'll tell you this, Ethel, that if that sap Archie Leverest had said one more word I'd have punched his snoot for a row of…"

…Those odd, those significant remarks that Linda had made to Slade on the morning of the murder about the smallness of the bullet—about the silence of the gun—if it had been the same gun. Valcour wondered exactly what would be the expert's report when it was cabled to him. Fingerprints were doubtful. But he had a strange premonition that somewhere, on the gun's wood stock…

One of the ship's officers had come in. He was a heavy-set man, scrupulously scrubbed, with a well-fed face and a professionally gallant manner. With him was a beefy, check-suited man, and two women whose dresses were almost lethal. They gathered at an opposite corner from Valcour, for bridge, gin fizzes, considerable high-pitched laughter, and much gallantry.

"Willie—look; Willie—no, don't turn now, wait until I tell you—it's the captain."

Willie looked. "Him?"

"Look at those buttons and those things on his shoulders."

"Him the captain? I hope we sink if he is. Look at that smirk on his pan. He's a bunch of tripe."

"Why, Willie Peterberg!"

"Yes, Mrs. Peterberg?"

"Isn't it lovely? I just can't get used yet to being called Mrs. Peterberg…"

…Who took the gun from Linda's room? Why had she herself taken it into her room? Valcour's eyes contracted a little. Had that bullet been meant for Arthur, or for that other, that so similar head, that equally tousled mop of coarse blond hair which belonged to Jess?…

"Well, well, well-well—well *well* well, well!"

Larry Stone was in the smoke room and coming towards him, sitting on the settee beside him, staring with faint covertness at him beneath the almost explosive energy of his greeting.

Valcour smiled and shook hands. "What are you drinking?" he said.

"The usual tonic—scotch and soda." Larry offered a cigar. "Smoke?"

"Only cigarettes, thanks." Valcour took out a pack and lighted one.

Larry leaned a little closer. "Look here," he said. "What are you with us for?"

Valcour smiled oddly. "Do you remember the Ancient Mariner?"

"Yes?"

"Well, I'm the albatross."

CHAPTER 18

Henry looked slyly at Wilbur Strange.

"I want a green tie," he said.

Henry was sitting on their cabin's settee. The pants to his dinner clothes were on. One low patent leather shoe was on. The thin, unmuscular upper half of his body was meagerly covered with a singlet.

"Lace your shoe and put on the other one," Wilbur said.

Wilbur Strange didn't turn. He was looking into a mirror fastened above a basin, fixing the bow in his black tie. His strong fingers were clever at it. He watched, in the mirror, Henry's untidy head, watched the crafty flicker in Henry's unclear eyes.

"I want a green tie."

"Don't shout."

Henry stood up. He opened a bag and rummaged in it. He found what he wanted and shoved it hurriedly into a trouser pocket when Wilbur wasn't looking. "Bet you get seasick," he said.

"Bet I don't."

"Well, you did last year coming back from England, and Arthur did." A spasm of fright contracted his features unpleasantly. His normally loose lower lip hung flaccid.

"*Arthur*—"

Wilbur moved with singular swiftness. He drew Henry down beside him on the settee—stared at him fixedly with his black and sultry eyes. "Arthur's O.K.," he said. "Arthur's in heaven."

Henry tried to turn his eyes away from Wilbur's. He couldn't. He felt himself weakly drifting into them along a strange slow current. "Heaven?" He repeated the word stupidly.

"Arthur is dead, but it's O.K., because he's in heaven."

"He can't be."

"He is."

"He can't be, because he's a thief." The pupils of Wilbur's eyes seemed to Henry to be all blackness, swallowing him. "They don't let thieves get into heaven. That old beast Gottschalk said so."

Gottschalk was the rather plumply efficient minister beneath whose guidance the Willett boys had lightly tasted religion during their early youth at Tuxedo.

"Gottschalk doesn't know what he's talking about." Wilbur's deep voice was monotonously quiet. "Arthur's in heaven."

Henry's lips were moist. "He's in hell," he said.

"There is no hell; the kind you mean."

"Then why is there a heaven?"

A steward knocked, came in, set a small silver tray with one cocktail down on a table. Wilbur signed the slip and the steward went out and closed the door.

"Give it to me," Henry said.

Wilbur picked up the cocktail. He went over to the basin and emptied it down the drain. "You can order as many of them as you like, but this is what will happen to them."

Henry stared at the basin stupidly. "I'm going to kill you," he said.

Wilbur had his back to him. He was gripping, with clenched hands, the edge of the basin. His face looked as if somebody had hashed it in. He didn't speak for a moment, and the cabin was very still—only the complaining creaks of the paneling, the faint pulsation from the engine, the thin clear thread of the first dinner bugle. He said: "I guess you win." He pressed a button and the silence lingered like dead and musty air until the steward rapped and came in.

"Another cocktail, steward."

"Yes, sir. Same kind?"

Wilbur looked at Henry and said, "Do you want the same kind?'

Henry was smiling brightly. He was very polite. "If you please, Wilbur, yes. I will have the same kind."

* * * *

The thin clear thread of the first dinner bugle drifted down the passage...

Linda got up from the settee. White chiffon clung to her slenderly, and from a shoulder strap white kid gardenias edged a trailing scarf. She stared in a mirror and felt uncomfortable at the amount of rouge on her cheeks. There was too much, but she felt that she needed it, any amount of it, to conceal that deadly pallor.

"Mr. Valcour is on board," she said.

Jess was sprawled in an armchair. He had a linen dressing gown on. His bigness filled it, and his thick muscular wrists stuck out from its sleeves. He looked at Linda; astonished, as he always was astonished, at her beauty. It would come to him freshly in waves, this astonishment, like something just discovered and very remarkable. And he would like, all over again, the idea of owning it.

"Is he?" It didn't seem to matter much to Jess whether Valcour were on board or not. Whether anybody was on board or not. Nothing ever mattered to him during those moments when he was experiencing so newly and so freshly one of those waves. Someday she was going to know that she loved him. If he battered it into her enough. There wasn't a bone in her body that he couldn't break beneath the pressure of his strength. He knew that. But it was like water. No matter how strong you were, you couldn't break water. He felt that hotness coming which generally came before a slow, creeping anger. The absurdity had just occurred to him that water might, in the end, be stronger than his strength. "How do you know he's on board?" he said.

"Larry stopped in while you were taking your bath. Larry said that Mr. Valcour is sitting at our table. We're at the purser's table." She continued staring at rouge. She knew that Jess was looking at her. At her back. She knew he wasn't paying the slightest attention to what she said.

"What's he on board for?"

"Larry says he says he's going to stay with us until the case is closed. He told Larry we needed protection until those letters were cleared up. Larry doesn't believe him." She put some powder on over the rouge. She sat down on the settee again. "You'd better dress."

"No hurry." Jess lighted a cigarette. She looked marvelous through the thin blue smoke. "Remember the lake up in Maine?" he said. She didn't answer him, and her eyes baffled him, and anger was again creeping slowly.

"You'd better dress, Jess."

He stood up. He had gotten from his chair the way a strong and clever animal might have, could an animal have sat in a chair. He went over and sat beside her on the settee. "Why did you take that gun into your room?" he said.

She wouldn't care so much if only he wouldn't smile that smile. It did something to his lips that made them look as if it were hurting them. She knew he wouldn't touch her while he had that smile. She felt she could kill herself right before his eyes while he had it on his lips and he wouldn't lift a finger to stop her. She felt like a fool for crying. She could still see the smile through the blurring wetness, see him sitting there with it, like a shaggy miserable rock, through the slow and deadly minute after minute of wetness, while he didn't raise a finger to touch her and the muscles all over his body were soft and weakly loose, and only his lips were bitterly stretched and tight…

He said: "You need fresh rouge on your face, Linda."

CHAPTER 19

Mr. Stanislaw ordered Cape Cods on the half shell, and surveyed the filling saloon. He had gray hair, peppered with black, a bland smile, a limitless fund of anecdotes, and not a single illusion left about life. The last ten of his fifty years had been passed in shuttling between New York and Bermuda as purser on the *Hamilton*.

The saloon was filling up with the usual crowd. This passage was, he knew, utterly devoid of celebrities; most passages on the *Hamilton* were utterly devoid of celebrities.

"Who's with me? he said to the waiter, when the man had brought the Cape Cods.

"One Valcour, one Strange, and five Stones, Mr. Stanislaw. Mostly related, I think."

"Good God!"

"Yes, sir."

"Any children?"

"No, Mr. Stanislaw."

"Well, that's a relief." He studied the menu with an apathetic eye, hoping as always that somewhere, somehow, he would find in it something that had never, never been on it before. He decoded the soups and pointed to an esoteric name. "Bring me a plate of that mutton broth."

"Yes, sir."

He was agreeably astonished and pleased to see two stiff shirt fronts heading for his table. Very few of the average run of the ship's passengers dressed for dinner, and about half of the few who did dress generally looked awkward and unaccustomed about it—but these two birds—He stood up. "Good-evening, gentlemen." He introduced himself. Valcour shook hands and presented Larry Stone.

"I understand there are four more of you, Mr. Stone."

"Yes, Mr. Stanislaw. I'm a nephew."

Now that was an odd thing to say. Mr. Stanislaw, from endless contacts with people who were exposed to the disarming influence of life at sea, was a very sound student of human nature. There was something the matter with Mr. Stone. Beneath the assured manner, beneath the easy smile, beneath that impeccable shirt front and the steadiness of his voice as he ordered dinner, Mr. Stanislaw knew there was something that bothered deeply. His first intuitive flash had been that Mr. Stone was a badly frightened young man, and his intuitive flashes were generally proven to be correct.

Mrs. Willett, in a black velvet compromise between a dinner dress, mourning, and the earlier years of the present century, reached the table and the chair on Mr. Stanislaw's right. She realized that Larry, with his usual thoughtfulness, had arranged to sit at her other side. She realized also that a Mr. Stanislaw was being presented to Mrs. "Stone." She clung to comforting banalities.

"The weather is very agreeable for a passage, Mr. Stanislaw.—Order for me, will you, dear Larry?—I have never made the Bermuda crossing. They tell me that the diagonal course across the Gulf Stream is usually rough regardless of the season. Do you find it so?"

Valcour discussed the merits of shark fin soup with Larry automatically, and stared with thoughtful eyes at Mrs. Willett. Never, since the very beginning of this curious case, had he felt so oppressed. There was a tension—nothing apparent—but deep beneath the surface; a shackled waiting for something very slow and very relentless, a flood of thick and death-giving lava drifting down upon them inch by inch...

"...yes, we have with us my two sons, Mr. Stanislaw, and my daughter-in-law. A Mr. Strange is with us, too. He is my younger son's tutor.—Still Burgundy, Larry, yes.—I am interested, Mr. Stanislaw, in beaches. I understand there is a good one just outside of Hamilton. Elco—Elto—"

"Elbow Beach, Mrs. Stone."

"Yes." Her remarkable eyes did not stop at him. They were through him, through the wall of the ship, the dark still night, to distant places hidden beneath a far-off lip of the obscure and restless sea. "I am looking for the sun."

Here's a weird bird, thought Mr. Stanislaw. It would be interesting to add her to his collection. She was too frightened, beneath her mottled skin and curious eyes (their largeness and slight protuberance disconcerted him, even though he knew perfectly well they weren't seeing him at all), and he could sense shock in her as accurately as some men with forked fruit-tree twigs could sense, deep underground, the presence of water. "I'd be careful about the sun while you're down there," he was saying. "It's more powerful than you think. The cold breeze from the sea makes the rays deceptive and people get pretty badly burned. Chief Justice Rutherford was saying to me only the last time we were in port that the hospital..."

Valcour could see them coming, down the last few steps of the curving stairs that led into the saloon; Henry and Jess and Wilbur Strange.

Henry's cheeks were flushed and there was a silly loose grin on his lips. He must have been giggling, because several people looked up at him as he passed their tables.

"I say there, Valcour!" Henry started to run. He reached the table in advance of Jess and Wilbur. "I'm going to sit beside you." He ignored the others and settled himself noisily in the seat next to Valcour, while Wilbur Strange took the chair on Henry's other side, and Jess came up more slowly and went over and shook hands with Mr. Stanislaw.

"My sons," Mrs. Willett said, "and Mr. Strange." Her look settled hesitantly on Wilbur—left him—returned—puzzled.

"Where's Linda?" Larry said to Jess.

Jess's eyes were little and his smile meant nothing at all. "She isn't coming to dinner," he said.

Valcour wondered just what was in back of that set queer smile of Jess's. "No, Mr. Stone," he went on talking, "the west coast of South America still remains an enigma to me. Our own side, yes. Pernambuco, Santos—the most delightful beach in the world—Rio, Rosario, Buenos Aires—you are familiar with the subway in B.A.? I could never shake off the impression when I rode on it that in some ghastly fashion I had got into a lady's boudoir by mistake." And Wilbur Strange was a chiseled rock. Where was the key to this whole miserable business, and what was the significance about Linda?...

Mr. Stanislaw, while vividly portraying for Mrs. Willett's benefit the lobsters one first selected and then ate out at Tom Moore's in Bermuda, could not keep his eyes from Henry. If the young buck had been his child, a series of good paddlings out in the woodshed—no, not quite that—what a singularly disagreeable face it was! Disagreeable wasn't the word, nor pathetic. Something between the two that touched but did not embrace them both.

"There is a place in Copenhagen where they also fete the lobster, Mr. Stanislaw. Perhaps you are familiar with it?" Mrs. Willett sipped Burgundy, and talked, and broke the food on her plate, and then ignored it utterly. "The lobsters themselves did not fascinate me so much as the forks that were used to eat them with—long, slender handles, not over an eighth of an inch in width, with a slight cleft at the end of them. There wasn't a smallest claw that didn't capitulate. The finger bowls, of course, had to be tubs." Henry was up to something. She knew the symptoms. For eighteen years she had known the symptoms. She tried to catch Wilbur's eye in order to signal to him. But Wilbur's eye seemed to be almost consciously avoiding hers. She was psychic to moods and Wilbur's—resignation? Could it be resignation? Revolt? Cold winds gathered in

her, and the line which held her to safe anchorage seemed very frayed…
"There is no season, is there, down in Bermuda? Social, not lobsters."

"None, really. Of course around Easter it's pretty well packed. The lilies are quite an attraction—fields of them all in bloom. Very lovely. I remember when…"

The tiresome, irritating talk went on and on, and Henry suddenly excused himself, with suspicious politeness, and left the table. She waited a moment for Wilbur to follow, but Wilbur made no move, just sat with his eyes fastened hard on his plate, and a dull flush creeping darkly up his face. She said to him directly, "Hadn't you better see what it is the dear boy wants, Wilbur? My younger son, Mr. Stanislaw, is a little capricious." Wilbur hadn't moved, but he was looking back at her with something queer in his eyes—desperate. "Well, Wilbur?"

He said, "It's no use."

Her lips took on the painful illusion of a smile. "I think—if you don't mind—" She was up, and the men were standing, too, and Larry had pushed back his chair to go with her. "No—thank you, dear Larry. I'll go alone, if you please. I am a woman of absurd impulses, Mr. Stanislaw. I am worried about the child's stomach. I will be back directly."

She was gone, and Valcour watched her quiet unhurried steps toward the curving stairs but he felt, like a sharp-pointed knife, the hurry that must be rattling in her heart. They sat down again. They talked. They ate. They ignored the dreadful whiteness of Wilbur Strange's sullen, damp, young face, and Mr. Stanislaw was finding small tastefulness in his coffee and his d'Oka cheese.

Even above the humming chatter of the filled saloon, they caught the curious garbled awkwardness of some commotion up above at the top of the curving stairs. Others had caught it, too, and one by one the voices were dying down. Larry, with suddenly startled eyes, was out of his chair and leaving them, before the commotion up above had completely subsided, as it did, and chatter hummed again.

"My brother," Jess was saying to Mr. Stanislaw, "is a little difficult to manage. Being the youngest, he has been thoroughly spoiled."

Mr. Stanislaw's smile was professionally bland; commotions were not good on ships. "Youngest? There are others?"

Jess stood up. He said abruptly: "There was one other." He excused himself and went away.

Valcour put down his empty coffee cup, stood up, and placed a hand on Wilbur's shoulder. "Finished?"

Wilbur got up and faced him. He said: "Quite."

They went off and Mr. Stanislaw endeavored to find a last moment of pleasure in the remaining bits of his d'Oka cheese. The waiter came over, and he said to him, "What was that rumpus up above?"

"It was right at the head of the stairs, Mr. Stanislaw."

"So I gathered."

"It was that young Stone here—the queer one. He'd taken off his black tie and put on a green one."

"Well?"

"Well, his old lady caught him at it proper, Mr. Stanislaw, and got him by the arm and tried to hold him back. He was dead set on coming down. He hit her a good crack on the snout, he did. Regular circus, it was."

Mr. Stanislaw closed his eyes. It was an involuntary habit of his whenever he encountered anything pitiably distressing. "Circuses," he said, "are supposed to be funny."

CHAPTER 20

He found her well forward on the boat deck, sitting on a slatted wooden bench at the foot of the starboard ladder leading to the officers' quarters. White chiffon dripped from the hem of a loose tweed coat and brushed upon silver slippers. Valcour could make little of her face in the night's enveloping darkness. Except for her, the forward portion of the deck was deserted—to the enigmatic, little, monstrous noises of a ship in darkness on the sea—geometric planes of black against a lesser black, the tracery of rigging, the pillared funnel swinging with such slow and sullen majesty across white stars.

"Cold up here, isn't it?" he said, and sat down on the bench beside her.

Linda drew the tweed coat closer. "They say that the water is the reverse of the air. When the air's cold, the water is warm, and vice versa."

Valcour could not gauge her voice. There was a detached preciseness about it. Her meaning was clear enough, and for a shocked moment his memory swung sharply back to another woman in a case he had handled several years ago, to that Mrs. Endicott—equally beautiful, but more complex and strange—who, too, had hinted at suicide, and from about whose neck he had been just in time to remove the noose… "The sea is friendless to the dead," he said.

She pulled herself back from great distances, focused her attention onto the present. She said quickly, "My remark held no significance, Mr. Valcour."

"Words rarely do. It's the manner in which they're spoken, their connotations. Why did you take that gun into your room?"

He could see her eyes through the semi-darkness, shocked wide with fright, while endless waves sang ripping past and canvas-covered metal guard lines fell and rose across a dead black sea.

"I think God curses prettiness," she said.

He felt a flare of interest, a plunging down to roots… "Because people consider it an end in itself?"

"Yes—yes." Her hand on his hand was over-hot. "It makes you a commodity. People get into trouble when they're pretty. It's like icing on a cake. If there isn't any on it, it's so much safer, so much happier for the cake."

He took a stab at being a bit obscure himself. "Isn't it all according to what you want? The cake gets eaten anyway."

"It isn't that," she said impatiently. "It's to keep on wanting it after you get it." Her laugh was a little too high. "The trouble with me, Mr. Valcour, is that I do."

He said rather gently, "And Mr. Willett doesn't?"

"I don't know." Her hand still clung to his hand, and she said quite suddenly: "I lied, Mr. Valcour. I lied. I didn't take that gun into my room at all."

His first reaction was of resignation to the utter fallibility of women when their emotions were concerned. Linda had been under oath, and had known it, when her testimony had been taken at the inquest. He smiled faintly. That was not his affair, and he could not visualize Dr. Ferris jumping on her for contempt of court, or for anything else. "Where did you take the gun?"

His voice blended carefully with her mood, tuned itself to the soft night wind, to the gentle busy ripping of the sea. Two lovers passed, not looking at them, not looking at anything, because there wasn't anything, just the two themselves, in all the world. Linda followed them with her eyes. "Love's for the very old," she said, "or for the very young." The lovers were swallowed amidship in darkness, the last lingering paleness of the girl's light coat slashed diagonally by the blackness of an arm, and Linda's voice was hard when she turned to Valcour and said, "My own age is thirty-three."

"I don't think it matters—heavens knows I'm not an expert—but I really don't think it matters."

"Mr. Valcour, it does." Her grip tightened on his hand. "You've got to be a fool to be in love. You mustn't think—ever—just be quite sense-less about it—as senseless as leaves are when they float on warm, quiet waters—you've got to live with your eyes shut."

"To such details as shaving?" he said pleasantly.

Her voice was sharp. "Yes—exactly—I think you know. I think you know a lot, Mr. Valcour. I'm not smart. I can't say things that are bright. I can't be witty. But I'm not stupid, Mr. Valcour. I feel things badly."

There was still a barrier between them. She was talking at him, and he at her. He could not get inside of her, as he wanted to. She wasn't, as yet, quite real. "Don't you think you over-analyze?"

"What is there left?"

He said, "As bad as that?"

"There's no steadiness about it. It comes in rushes."

"Hate?"

The word struck her as a novelty. She seemed to examine it from all angles. "Isn't it about the same thing?"

"As love?"

"Can't you lump them all together? One word could cover the lot. I think hell would be a good word, Mr. Valcour, to cover the lot."

"Where did you take the gun?"

"I left it—I saw it—that is to say, he—"

"Linda."

Both of them started at the voice, and Jess joined them from the ladder's shadow, and Linda's fingers on Valcour's hand were a sharp contracting vise.

"You frightened me, Jess."

Jess ignored her completely. He said to Valcour, "Linda's been upset the last few days. I'm going to take her to bed." Valcour could feel her fingers loosening—slipping—there was reluctance in their going.

"Won't you sit up here with us for a while longer, Jess?" Her voice was pitifully thin. "I like it up here."

"If you wish." Jess sat down. He put an arm around Linda. His voice did not reflect his smile. "You miss a lot, Mr. Valcour, by not being married," he said.

CHAPTER 21

The first of the cablegrams from headquarters which Valcour received during the Willetts' brief stay in Bermuda was delivered to him in his room at the Hamilton Hotel on the morning of their arrival. Valcour decoded it.

The cable read (as the Police Department had lots of money) at length: All known tests applied. Never was any writing on paper at all. Your surmise as to lack of slightest pen or pencil pressure correct. Smart boy that you are. The lads and lassies of the homicide squad send lots of love and hope you choke on Planter's Punches. Don't get run over by the street cars even if there aren't any. Signed: Peter.

Valcour smiled and tore the message up. Peter, who was an analytic chemist of no small repute, was the departmental joker. The courtyard beneath Valcour's windows was white with sunshine and its edge lush green with hot splashes of flame-colored flowers. He wondered absently what their names were and whether they had any smell. It was funny, all right, for Peter. Peter could joke. It didn't mean anything to Peter. It was common-place to him—a routine business, casually of interest in an academic way, focused in the spotlight for its short moment until another case would come along, and the spotlight moved—but to that tired old tragic woman down the hall…

There never was any writing on the paper at all. (How brilliant green was in the sunlight down here, and how hot the flame red flowers!) There were two pictures that could each so easily be drawn. The first was simply that Mrs. Willett had never received any message at all. She had folded a sheet of paper, concealed it in her maroon velvet bodice, handed it to him and said—after he had remarked upon its blankness, "Then the ink has been chemically treated." As simple as that. And Valcour inclined rather strongly in this belief until that miserable and shocking moment after their return to New York when Mrs. Willett was suddenly dead from poison.

The second picture was more complex. It opened with Mrs. Willett unfolding the paper and staring at the single word: "Soon." It continued with heavens knows what of fear and misery and worry that there must have been in her weary heart—with her leaving the paper on her dresser while she bathed in the adjoining bathroom—with the swift, silent entrance into her bedroom of the sender of that message, and the substitution in its place of a similarly folded sheet of blank paper. That sender. The "extortionist"? Valcour felt that less than ever did that mystical extortionist figure fit in. It was entirely too much to believe that any stranger to that camp and to that household would have been capable of such very well-timed and such competent flittings.

Valcour stared idly at a printed card on the room's desk. It informed him, among several things, that Bermuda's drinking water was the finest in the world, that the rain it consisted of was gathered from the limestone roofs and stored in cisterns, and that people would please, in consequence, refrain from throwing cigarette hurts and kindred litter from the windows, etc., etc., etc… He lifted the receiver from the telephone and ordered a bottle of Lithia water and cracked ice.

And if you did block out this figure of the threat-note-writing extortionist from the picture, who took his place? Larry? Linda? Wilbur Strange? The air was soft and warm through the opened windows and perfumed with frail scents of endless flowers. Henry? Jess? Fratricide was curiously rare.

The mirror informed him that, with any sort of luck, he wouldn't have to shave again before evening. Did he or did he not look like a complete damn fool in that red tie? Always, in warmness and sunshine and the lazy loveliness of these peaceful world-divorced islands in their emerald sea, he had a mania for wearing white-and-tan rubber-soled oxfords and a bright red tie. He did look like a damn fool. He left it on.

Slade?

You breathed it into you with every lungful of the air. This blessed romantic something. It did things to your head. It took the years from your back until layer by layer you were a fool again. You weren't afraid any more. Happiness quite suddenly lost its silliness and you weren't afraid of it any more. Women could do that to you, Valcour supposed. Well, he thanked God, so could Bermuda.

He said, "Come in!" to a lazy rap, and watched a colored bellboy drift like a slow-motion picture to a table and deposit a bottle of Lithia water and a pitcher of cracked ice on its top. A soft-spoken English accent asked: "Will there be anything else, sir?" and then, having been tipped, the boy was gone both like and in a trance.

Valcour stared at the Lithia water. He said, "To hell with it." He took one apologetic look of dissipating doubt at his red, red tie, then left the room, and inch by inch descended in a big and dreamlike elevator to the lobby. He passed through its sunlit whiteness into a large and dim cool bar. He ordered one cable blank and one Planter's Punch.

"Dear Peter," [he wrote] *"here is how."*

* * * *

The second cablegram was longer. It didn't come from Peter. There was nothing flip in it, and Valcour could picture the lean-faced, spectacled head of the Special Investigations Bureau as he had dictated it. The bell captain had given it to Valcour as he had left the bar and gone into the lobby. He had sat down in a chair, read the cablegram, torn it up, and was digesting its very unsatisfactory contents when Larry spotted him and came over. Larry had a bathing bag in his hand.

"Want to come for a swim, Mr. Valcour? The whole troupe's going. Chance of a lifetime."

"If you don't mind waiting until I get my suit—"

"Not a bit. Are you bicycling, or will you join the weaker of us in a canopied and tasseled hack?"

"Bicycling by all means, Mr. Stone. Wherever else in the world do you get a chance at it? You didn't know that I used to be a champion rider, did you? Well, neither did I." Valcour turned back for an instant. "By the way, is Wilbur Strange included in the 'troupe'?"

Larry looked at him oddly.

"Yes," he said.

The sharp curve to the left—then coasting down the hill with small bells jangling, using the left-side-of-the-road traffic—Linda and Jess and Henry and Wilbur, all with Valcour on bicycles flying down the steep sun-blazing hill, and then sharp again to its left at the base along the dusty, small-buildinged, waterfront street with its coral-baited shops and ivories, its shipping offices and merchant houses and ship chandlers smelling of the seven seas, its sun-tanned tourists (you could gauge almost to a day how long they had been there by the varying complexion stages from shrimp pink to chocolate) and its horse-drawn drays, while trotting smartly behind them was the victoria with Larry Stone and Mrs. Willett beneath its cream white, tasseled linen top.

White coral road swung up and down through shrubs of green, and walls of green, and distant green, all splashed with lazy flowers beneath a hot blue sky, for several miles, then down a lane, and there beneath them was white sand that edged a reef-guarded segment of a clear and emerald sea.

Sand rippled through Valcour's fingers and he said, "Your family is living, Mr. Strange?"

"I have no family, Mr. Valcour."

Valcour smiled pleasantly. "Isn't that a little equivocal? Am I to gather from it that your parents, your nearer relatives, are physically dead, or that you choose to consider them so?"

"I don't know." Wilbur's muscular and well-modeled flesh was pearl white in the blazing sun. "I've never been much good," he said.

"The breaks haven't been very lucky?"

"Not until this one. And now this one isn't so lucky."

"Where were you born, Mr. Strange?"

"Vermont—Burlington."

"You went to school there?"

"Yes "

"College?"

"For a while." His face flushed slowly. "I suppose you'll look that up."

"If it becomes necessary, and unless you prefer to tell me."

"What would it have to do with this business, Mr. Valcour?"

"Because I believe, Mr. Strange, that the answer to this curious case will never be found in the present."

"Well?" Young Strange's face was leaden again, very gray, very tense.

"What were you expelled from college for?" Valcour said.

The eyes flickered for a second. "I was given an opportunity to re-sign. I took it."

Valcour shrugged. His look drifted from Henry, who was shouting his way through the gentle surf with Jess and Larry and Linda, then on to Mrs. Willett, cool in white linen in a beach chair, with lids shut quietly over weary eyes and her face losing a little of its frozen look under the bright clear warmth.

"Your introduction to Mrs. Willett came about in what way, Mr. Strange?"

"An advertisement."

"Mrs. Willett advertised?"

"No. I advertised."

"For the job of tutor?"

Wilbur's voice was queer. There was a palpable and astonishing tone of defiance in it. "No," he said. "I advertised for a mother who might be interested in having someone save her son."

CHAPTER 22

It was an infant, as the age of turtles goes, having on its little back only the worldly experience of seventy brief years. It rested in the center of a stone-flagged inner court of a small hotel just midway down the hill between the Hamilton and the waterfront, and philosophically chewed off flame-scarlet petals from a flower.

Four competently and happily intoxicated tourists were fascinated with him from a table set in the lush and tropic foliage of the court's outer edge. Valcour recognized them as the contract-playing quartet in the smoke room of the *Hamilton* on the trip down. He was sitting with Larry at a marble-topped table in one of the bowered alcoves, sipping a Bacardi cocktail, watching the indifferent turtle, and thinking what a pity it was that the odorous beauty and contentment of this late afternoon must have, for bitter undercurrent, such a stupid thing as murder.

It was forever astonishing him: the specious arguments or violent flares of emotion by which so many people would arrive at murder, would seize it as a solution to their special problem. And it never was. He imagined that even in the earliest days, before the complex machinery of justice had been built, murder at best must have been an unsatisfactory makeshift. The act in itself was of such comparative unimportance, certainly so to the victim, who would be dead, and nothing mattered to the final nothingness of being dead; but to those who still lived on… "Mr. Stone," he said, "I have asked you to meet me here apart from the others for two reasons. I believe that bluntness is less brutal than suspense. The first reason is to inform you that we return on the *Arcadian* which sails in the morning. The other one is to advise you that upon our arrival in New York you will at once be placed under arrest."

A dipsomaniac in an adjoining alcove was wearily dropping china plates on stone flagging, and the four young tourists were concentrating their over-earnest attention on him. The turtle, with hundreds of years of leisure to do it in, was placidly nibbling on his second petal of deep red flame. The flushing quadrangle of sky was melting into unearthly tints, and Larry's white young checks were death. "That's all sort of foolish, isn't it?" he said.

Valcour was quietly evasive. He took another sip of his Bacardi cocktail. He said, "I cannot say."

"But you must say something. You can't just come out and say things like that, Mr. Valcour, without saying something. You can't say a foolish thing like that and not say something."

"Steady, Mr. Stone."

Larry finished his drink. He winced slightly as their neighboring dipsomaniac dropped and shattered, with patient care, another plate. He said more calmly, "What's it all about, Mr. Valcour?"

"Let us go back to the day when we left the camp for New York. You packed your own trunks, did you not?"

"Yes, Mr. Valcour."

"There were two?"

"Two."

"They were shipped to the Plaza and both brought up to your room?"

"Yes, Mr. Valcour."

"You repacked them there, putting such things as you would need into the smaller one for this trip, and checking the larger one to be held for you at the hotel?"

"Yes."

"You will join me in another? Of course.—Two more Bacardis, waiter.—Were you assisted at all in this packing, Mr. Stone?"

"No, Mr. Valcour, I always pack. I've always packed my own things."

"Your broker informs us that your account was wiped out entirely by the recent collapse of the stock market."

"When did you find that out?"

"This afternoon."

"What?"

"There are cables, Mr. Stone."

"That's right." The idea was mildly stunning. Any idea was stunning in the dull achingness of Larry's mind. "You sort of feel so detached here. More than Europe. Cut off and so safe from things." He said with peculiar earnestness: "I guess there isn't any place on earth, Mr. Valcour, where a person's really safe from things."

"Would you care to tell me your financial position?"

"At present?"

"That, and what it has been generally. I'm not vulgarly curious. I like you." For a ghastly second Valcour was afraid that Larry was going to cry. In police work, more perhaps than in any other profession, did you run into men who would suddenly start to cry. The waiter, softly sliding toward them through mauve shadows of the thick dark green, with two splendidly frosted clear Bacardis on a tray… "Get on the outside of one of these, Mr. Stone," he said.

…"Waiter, *garçon*, come here, my pet!"

The two young couples waved eight hands high up in the air, and one of them said, "I bet we look like Rinehart's Miracle."

"Or Peter Pan."

"Isn't he screaming, Peggy? He wants green turtle soup. Oscar wants green turtle soup."

"The name is Freddy, my good woman."

"He can't have it. I've been sitting here watching that darling, dear sweet little turtle eating hours for flowers and flowers and Oscar can't have it." A determined gleam came into Peggy's eye as she added, "*I'm going to have it.*"

"I haven't any financial position, Mr. Valcour. It's true that I've been wiped out. I never was rich. There was enough from my father's estate to make a pleasant income for a single man. It was turned over to me when I came of age." Lights were turned on in the dark and lush green shrubs, and a single star was impudently brilliant in a still pale sky. The turtle had eaten up its flame-red flower and with thoughtful steps was moving from the court. "I wanted to get established financially—independently."

"When did you start playing the market?"

"June—July—somewhere in June or July."

"Things broke badly right off the bat?"

"Yes, Mr. Valcour."

"Here's a simple outline of how they are looking at things, Mr. Stone. The motive rests on your need of ready money. The opportunity is palpable—you were aware of Mrs. Willett's movements, you were in a position to write and mail her the threat letters, you were well able to slip the final letter in among her mail and to substitute a blank sheet of paper for it later when she left it on her dresser, you were in a position to have shot Arthur. A weapon was found by you whose rifling leaves comparable marks on a bullet fired from it as were left on the bullet that lodged in Arthur's head, and there are on the weapon no other fingerprints than your own." Valcour repeated softly, "The motive, the opportunity, and the weapon of the crime. Yes, they have a good case against you, Mr. Stone."

"I didn't kill Arthur."

"They are under the impression that you did." Valcour's voice grew delicately formal. "I dare say that you can obtain competent legal advice here, Mr. Stone, as to your rights concerning extradition proceedings if you choose to insist upon them. They will serve no further purpose than the added anxiety of delay. Whereas if you accede to my suggestion that we sail on the *Arcadian* in the morning I can offer you a complete avoidance of the little unpleasantnesses attendant on a formal arrest until we are in New York. The matter will then be out of my hands."

"Have we got to tell Kate?" Larry said.

"It has been my experience, Mr. Stone, that evasion or subterfuge have caused more pain than an immediate clear statement of fact. We recover more rapidly from one swift sharp shock than from any nerve-draining and protracted period of innuendo."

The turtle was gone, the four young tourists were gone, the dipsomaniac's nose was pressed flat on the dishless marble table top in sleep, and five more stars were dripping in the sky.

"Why should I kill Arthur to get money?" Larry said.

"They don't think you did. They think you killed him because he saw you take it, and they reason that if he'd told about it, that would have linked you up with the extortion letters, which would in turn have unquestionably alienated your aunt."

"Arthur saw me take what, please, Mr. Valcour?" Golly, how cold it was! But Mr. Valcour didn't seem to be cold. That dark waiter standing over there in green darkness didn't seem to be cold.

"The twenty thousand dollars, Mr. Stone."

"Well?"

"They found it in your trunk. The trunk you checked at the Plaza."

"I see."

Valcour said softly, "Tell me whom you suspect of having planted that money in your trunk."

"That, Mr. Valcour?" Larry's eyes were sick. "Oh, I did that."

CHAPTER 23

The tall French windows of the grill were wide-open to a moon-drenched terrace of scented beauty, and shaded lamps on tables edging the large oblong dance floor were an agreeable and flattering glow. Musicians from the States, on a platform at the room's end, played endless fox trots endlessly, and Mrs. Willett, severe in satin, sipped champagne mechanically from a thin, chilled glass.

"It is not like Larry to get drunk," she said. "This absurd charge, Mr. Valcour, surely it will not be pressed?"

They stared at Larry, at his beady paleness, uncertainly making his way toward a terrace window.

"One must appreciate the state attorney's point of view," Valcour said. "Unquestionably, Mrs. Willett, he has a case."

"The money was mine. The money is mine. I give it freely." Mrs. Willett's large eyes made a pitiful stab at domination. "Whatever nonsense attended the discovery of the money, there has been no theft."

"Unfortunately Mr. Stone admits one."

"It is impossible to steal what is given you."

"That is only one detail in the picture, Mrs. Willett. It is the broader subject that we have to worry about."

"This stupid charge of murder?"

"There is danger connected with any murder charge, whether it is stupidly made or not. I will be frank with you. I shall not say that your nephew is not the type one associates with a killer, because there are as many types of killers as there are of people." He tried, by smiling, to lighten some of the heaviness in those tired old eyes. "I could show you photographs of what would seem to be the most charming men and yet all of whom were executed for their crimes. No, Mrs. Willett, the capacity for theft or murder is something out of sight within a man and is not stamped upon his surface. It is simply that I have come to know your nephew, to like him. I believe him incapable either of that theft or of that graver crime. My belief, however, is not of great value to him. I am a detective, and not the state's attorney."

Under a soft hypnotic beat of music, a surface chatter of the pleasure-heavy room, Mrs. Willett's voice pressed like cold iron. "You will clear him of this," she said, "and I will thank you."

"I'm afraid there is only one way of doing so."

"Yes, Mr. Valcour?"

"That is by our finding the proper person to take his place."

"Of course." She sipped champagne. Her eyes searched negligently through the dancers, rested on Jess's strong and expressionless features and Linda too tight in his arms. Jess ought to take some lessons. But did lessons do any good? You danced or you didn't. Larry, for instance. Even drunk, Larry danced. He had the feel for rhythm. Wilbur and Henry at the end of the table. Talking. The waiter was filling Henry's glass again. There was that stuff that kept her hair smooth. She had tried it on Henry's hair, but it hadn't kept his hair smooth. She said again: "Of course."

A night clerk was standing in the entrance archway. Valcour could see him looking toward their table and indicating it to a bellboy. He wondered what this latest cablegram would be, and stared at it curiously as the bellboy offered it to Mrs. Willett. She opened it, read it, folded it minutely, and kept it in her hand. "From Slade,' she said. "He informs me that the town house is ready." She drank from her glass deeply, then took a napkin and wiped a spot where some champagne had spilled upon her dress. "I am incurably nervous about wired messages. My husband's death was announced by one. A motor accident in the Pyrenees. He was killed instantly."

The music stopped on the thin wail of a muted trumpet and chatter surged above it, and Jess and Linda were sitting at the table, with Henry saying to her, "The next dance is mine. I'm going to have the next dance with Linda. When does this beastly music start? You're going to dance next with me, Linda." They were looking at each other, the two women, across the blossom-sprayed table, and Linda's chilled face slowly softened with unresisting pity. She managed to smile at Henry and said, "Thank you," and caught as a faint echo from the older woman's badly penciled lips, "I thank you, too."

Jess came over beside Valcour and said, for the tenth time that night, "There must be some way of fixing this." He was looking at Larry, standing in one of the French windows, staring out onto the moon-clear terrace flowering with lovers—with old lovers—young lovers—new lovers—and those whose love was being found again. Jess mentioned the most prominent criminal lawyer in the country. "I've already cabled and retained him for Larry," he said.

"A very wise move, Mr. Willett."

"Look at that little damned fool."

The music had started and Henry had already managed to break the loop by which Linda held up her train. Her incredible loveliness was marble too highly rouged, and her eyes were senselessly bright above lips strained into the semblance of a smile. The floor was still quite empty. Few of the couples had drifted back yet from the terrace or had left their tables, and Henry's grin as he pushed Linda jerkily about the dance floor's outer rim was impartially bestowed upon those who were sitting down. A few grinned back at them, but there were some who started to, and then did not. A doctor who was sitting at one of the tables stared at Linda, started to rise, shrugged, and then sat down again. The four contract players from the *Hamilton* accepted Henry as a sight and frankly said so.

—"Listen, Oscar, I can't bear it. Peggy says it's Freud's dream come true…"

"*Deep night*" (sang one of the saxophonists through a megaphone), "*stars in the sky-yy above—Moon bright—lighting our place of love…*"

"Wilbur, my dear boy, go over and cut in." Mrs. Willett's mottled cheeks were a travesty under geranium rouge.

"*Night winds—seem to have gone to rest—Two eyes—brightly with love are gleaming—Come to my arms, my dear one, my sweetheart, my own*—Chees' Bill," the singer shot sideways to the pianist, "get it?—*Vow that you'll love me always and be mine alo-one…*"

"I'm cutting in, Henry." Wilbur kept walking, his hand on Henry's jerking shoulder.

"Go away. Go sit on a tack."

"I'm cutting in."

"*Deep night—whispering tree-ees above…*"

"Oscar—he's tripped her! Oh, my God, Oscar, he's—"

"Shut up, Peg."

"*Kind night, bringing you nearer, dearer and dearer—Deep…*"

The crack of Henry's fist on Wilbur's chin was quite clear, and Valcour was already helping Linda to her feet and steadying her as she said, "I'm quite all right—it's quite all right," and she felt herself being hurried toward the door, and Valcour's arm was secure about her—so impersonally secure about her—and with bewildering suddenness they were knotted, very pale, very strained, in the grill's foyer and Jess was talking rapidly to the head waiter and a yellow bill flashed—and Mrs. Willett, poised magnificently as a charred sheet of paper before a torch can crumple it to ash, said, "It is time for bed."

In reviewing the case after its tragic close it did not surprise Valcour that the conclusive clue should not only have been ignored, but missed entirely during that wretched scene on the dance floor in the grill. He was handed a cablegram by the night clerk as he passed the desk. He put it in his pocket and went with the others to the elevators, where he said good-night.

"Not turning in?" Jess said, through set white lips.

"Not yet."

Valcour went outside onto the hotel's deep and long piazza. His heart felt sick and the whole miserable dance business of Henry and Linda and Wilbur had left a bad taste in his mouth, and he knew that Mrs. Willett's beaten eyes were going to stay with him for life. He walked around and got his bicycle from the racked room, lighted its kerosene lamp, and coasted slowly downhill to the waterfront. He wanted some air before he opened that cablegram in his pocket. He wanted some air before he did anything or thought of anything at all.

The quietness and the stillness…and the coral road was white with moonlight, and Mrs. Willett's face came sharply back as she had said to him that morning out on the sands at Elbow Beach: "So still here, Mr. Valcour. It was difficult for me to realize at the hotel that we were in a city. I could hear birds singing through the opened window quite plainly. There should be magic. Some formula by which one could command arrested motion. I think I would have chosen that single hour, and I would sit forever, and never move again, beside that opened window through which birds were singing, and look at sunshine on the garden of that sheltered court."

What a pity it was, Valcour thought, that the hurry and congestion of present-day traffic had forced cycling against the wall. There was such fun in it, such silly soothingness to sift like this, a happy shadow through the obscure beauties of this star-hung and enchanted land. A girl in evening dress, kept snug with wooden clippers, and a boy cycled drifting, laughing, past, and light-chinked shutters beneath a limestone roof of a waterfront cafe were appealingly mysterious with snatches of a mellow Negro song.

Larry wouldn't make any trouble, of course. Larry wasn't the type that made trouble, and the voyage back on the *Arcadian* would be an uneventful if a disagreeable strain. Who was it Larry thought had planted the twenty thousand dollars in his trunk, and was the murder of Arthur really dovetailed with that theft? How bright and clear and still the moonlight was on this coral ribbon banked with soft smelling green!

Valcour dismounted and took the cablegram from his pocket. He opened it, held it near the bicycle's kerosene lamp, decoded it mentally, and read:

"Further microscopic examination of gun stock upon your recent advices disclosed traces of face powder and rouge.

Justifiable to deduce that stock when gun was fired had been pressed against a woman's cheek. State's attorney deeply upset and holding case in abeyance until your arrival with Willetts on Arcadian."

Valcour turned the bicycle and pedaled slowly back along the coral road. Its fragrant loveliness and beauty were blind and dead. A woman's cheek obscured them. A woman's cheek tight-pressed against the wood stock of that gun.

CHAPTER 24

The Willett home on Fifth Avenue and the Sixties, in New York City, was one of the few brownstone houses that the apartment builders had still failed to acquire. It was a big, solid building with a five-window frontage on Central Park, high ceilings, electrified gas chandeliers, and rather frightful shadow-boxed paintings that had been expensively acquired by Allenby Mortimer Willett during his frequent spurts through Europe in the Eighteen-nineties.

Mrs. Willett's bedroom was on the second floor front, and took in the house's entire width. A six-bracketed ormolu chandelier hung from a modeled plaster circlet on the high ceiling's center. The plaster modeling was an indiscriminate clustering of fruits and flowers, with no accurate regard either to the compatibility or season, and from it on faint clouds were strung to the room's four corners a spatter of still fainter and dumpling angels. Mortimer Allenby Willett had thought it magnificent. As for Mrs. Willett, she had neither then, nor did she now, care.

A Wilton carpet was thick beneath massive mahogany furniture splayed with deeply carved designs. The dominant note was a great mahogany double bed, the head of which was an elegant example of what the wood-carving guild could really do when it set its mind about it. Mrs. Willett, looking washed-out and pale, was in that bed.

It had been her longed-for goal, that bed, upon the *Arcadian's* docking and clearing by the port authorities. She hadn't used it very much during the past ten or twelve years, and she had forgotten how roomy, how yielding, how really comfortable it was. It was good to be in it again. It was good to be home again, for that was what this house with its ungainly extravagances of an earlier age had signified to her always. Home. During all the fruitless and erratic wanderings of the past endless years, this brownstone building with its solid, substantial, ugly face serenely fronting on Fifth Avenue had always stood waiting for her in the background.

Saturated with ghosts. Every tread of its solid oak stairs, every inch of its parquet flooring, every room, every closet, every drawer, was saturated with ghosts. She had gone through its rooms (before sinking into the blessed and enveloping security of that bed), through its closets and its drawers, fingering things, collecting a few things for immediate use in her room, meeting forgotten ones all over again, complimenting Slade—who had been oddly pale and nervous—on the efficiency with which he had assembled so competent a staff, and on the immaculate condition that everything was in.

Jess and Larry and Mr. Valcour had gone off at once with the commanding officer of the detective division, who had met them at the dock. She understood they were going to Police Headquarters, and Mr. Valcour had assured her with a peculiar and an almost formal gravity that there was little doubt but that Larry would be released on bond, in view of certain recent developments in the case. It was that statement which had shrunken her a little: in view of certain recent developments in the case.

Indian summer, she supposed it was, that made the breeze so temperate which blew in through an opened window from across the park. Traffic from the avenue below was pleasant to hear. The individualistic blending of noises which, from miles and miles around, signified New York. It had been born in her blood, the love of it, and its understanding. It seemed to her that for years and years she had missed it. And now she had it back again.

That same French marble clock on the mantel-piece. Allenby had picked out that clock twenty—thirty—thirty-five years ago in Paris. She remembered the shop—dingy, little, clattering with clocks. Allenby himself had placed it on the mantelpiece, and nobody had moved it since. It was incredible that they should ever have both looked at its face, as she alone was looking at its face…

Linda and Henry and Wilbur had come home with her from the dock. They were somewhere about the house. Linda. What a family they must seem to Linda! What a pity it was she couldn't go to the girl and say: "Dear child, here is my experience. I lay it at your feet. Dissect it, and govern your path accordingly." It wouldn't do. Experience was valueless unless one had acquired it of one's self. And by then it was too late for use. Linda's marriage with Jess must adjust itself. It would either do so of its own accord or it would break apart upon the rocks. No outer hand could guide its ship. Unless (Mrs. Willett's eyes closed sharply) one were to smooth the sea…

Henry had wanted to go to a movie, and had been pretty terrible about it, and Linda had wanted to go out for a walk in the park. But they couldn't. They couldn't leave the house because of that noncommittal-faced detective who was sitting on a marble bench by the iron-grilled plate-glass door. No one, because of him, could leave the house at all.

People were so silly, with all the elaborate and complicated motions which they went through. Alexander the Great really had the right idea, when he had simply taken his sword and sliced from the yoke of King Gordius's chariot that tight hard knot. It was stupid to try and loosen things. Lifetimes were wasted at it, and so much, so very much that was of true importance was passed by either from necessity or blindness during the lengthy process.

The French marble clock struck noon. A maid would be bringing her some lunch in an hour. What had the maid said her name was? Simpson. That was it. A very competent, thin, middle-aged woman. She had struck Mrs. Willett as being somewhat superior to her station. Intellectually. Not from anything that Simpson had said, but the feeling was there about her.

One of the Avenue's buses rumbled by, backfiring loudly, and for a moment Mrs. Willett did not hear the rapping on her door. Simpson? No. Mrs. Willett was sensitive to raps. She found this one puzzling her. There was something about it that was oddly disturbing.

She said: "Yes?"

The door opened rather swiftly. The muscles in her throat contracted into hard and paralyzing knots. She realized she had tried, but had failed, to scream. By exerting an almost superhuman effort she did manage to say: "Oh—come in."

CHAPTER 25

The motor swung from Centre Street on into the broad traffic-streamed length of Lafayette. Valcour leaned back against cushions and moodily observed the street's shoddy air of past splendor. Jess Willett and Larry were on the seat beside him. Larry was sitting quiet. Tight-lipped and still. Getting the reaction from the nervous strain of the past few days.

Jess wanted to talk. He wanted to get things straightened out. "What's the next move now, Mr. Valcour?" he said.

Valcour was vague. "Things will happen pretty soon now, Mr. Willett."

"Happen? What's going to happen?"

"I mean that the investigation can be definitely directed along a certain line."

"What line, Mr. Valcour?"

"I regret that I am not at liberty to tell you."

They slid into the clatter of Fourth Avenue and shortly were halted by cross traffic at Union Square.

"You had quite a conference with the commissioner," Jess said.

"Quite a conference, Mr. Willett."

Jess was silent for several blocks. Then he said, "Will we have to go back up to camp again, or is the case going to be handled from down here?"

"That I could not say. Temporarily, the state's attorney is willing that the investigation be pushed from down here."

The lower wholesale district of Fifth Avenue was sliding past. They skirted Madison Square and Valcour leaned forward to look at the clock on the Metropolitan Tower. Its hands lacked ten minutes of noon.

"I hope there's some Scotch in the house," Larry said. He smiled faintly and added, "There's nothing in the bond about not drinking Scotch is there, Mr. Valcour?"

Valcour smiled back at him. "Not a thing, Mr. Stone." They said nothing further. Each sat with his private and special thoughts—figuring—planning—dissecting—while the car in swift spurts covered the shopping district with its magnificent houses of commerce and its sidewalks massed thick with their noonday crowds, and shortly the green of Central Park was on their left and they were drawing up at the curb before the iron-grilled entrance to the Willett home.

Valcour stopped in the entrance hall to talk with Detective Jensen, who had got up from the marble bench and opened the door to let them in. Jess and Larry were in an adjoining coat room, taking off their things.

"Everything all right, Jensen?"

"Yes, Lieutenant."

"Anybody try to go out?"

"That young Mrs. Willett was after wanting to go for a walk in the park. Her face was like a bit of chalk with two red spots on it, Lieutenant. And that hell-cat of a son had it in his head to be off to the talkies. I've a good kick on my right shin and it hurts me yet."

"I have arranged to have a man relieve you at one o'clock."

"And I'll be damned glad of that, sir. Right up to me did he come, as nice and polite as you please. 'I am awfully sorry, officer,' he says, 'that you will not permit me to go to the talkies,' and gave me a kick on the shin."

"Who else is here with you, Jensen?"

"Simpson, sir. She's being Mrs. Willett's maid. Then there's Blaine, who can't make up his mind whether he's a second man or a footman, and they got a blimp by the name of Harris keeping watch down below at the servants' entrance."

Jess and Larry came back into the entrance hall and Jess said, "I say, Mr. Valcour, is there any need of this detective staying here, now that Larry's out on bond? It's not exactly the pleasantest thing in the world for the family."

"I am afraid, Mr. Willett, that that is the fault of the family."

"You're rather ambiguous."

"On the contrary. If there were less evasion, if a frank and clear statement of facts were made by those concerned in this case, it would soon be closed."

"Evasion? Who's evasive?"

"Your mother, yourself, Mr. Stone, Mr. Strange, and your wife."

Jess's laugh was disagreeable. "You'll forgive me if I fail to see it. And while you're about it, why not include Henry and Slade?"

"It is my purpose, Mr. Willett, to interview Slade directly." Jess's eyes were suddenly little. His voice lost its unpleasant harshness and was quite soft, and its Boston accent more pronounced. "In regard to what, Mr. Valcour?"

"In regard to a communication which he sent to headquarters while we were down in Bermuda."

"So that's what the conference with the commissioner was about."

"Among a few other things, yes, that is what it was about." They stared at each other deliberately, and their eyes did not move until Larry said suddenly: "Who is that woman on the stairs?"

They turned sharply and faced the stairs. Simpson was hurrying down their dark oak treads, hurrying dangerously, her plain black maid's costume blotted out against the broad dark stairs, only her face and starched cap and small apron dreadfully white. She hurried directly up to Valcour and said, "Come upstairs with me at once, Lieutenant."

"What is it, Simpson?"

"Mrs. Willett."

"Kate?" Larry's voice was sharp. He was already running rapidly towards the stairs, with a stark and dreadful fear in his heart.

"She's hurt." Simpson's voice was nervous. "I picked her up and put her back upon the bed."

CHAPTER 26

The mottles on Mrs. Willett's white face were shockingly clear, and her prominent eyes had a flat, stunned look. A blue welt was noticeable on her forehead.

"Kate—I say there, Kate, old girl." Larry was over at the bed beside her, pressing her large-knuckled fingers, and his lips were as bloodless as hers.

She said: "So stupid of me, my dear boy. I got out of bed and tripped. My head struck the foot of the bed. I foolishly fainted."

Valcour did not believe it. Not for one minute did he believe that simple and logical statement issued by Mrs. Willett in her forced and uneven voice. He looked at Simpson, and she imperceptibly shook her head.

Jess was beside the bed, too. Towering beside it in his bigness. "I'll telephone Dr. Willmott," he said.

"Nonsense. You will do nothing of the sort. There is witch hazel in the medicine locker in the bathroom. Simpson will fix a cold application, and I will be down to join you at lunch." Color was coming slowly again into Larry's face. "I'm all right, by the way, Kate," he said. "They've turned me loose on bond. The Peril of the Pampas is loose again on bond."

"Dear Larry." She caught and pressed his covering hand. She liked his hand, the feel of it, its fresh coolness and kind young strength. She looked at Valcour and gave him one of her rare and bewildering smiles. "You are our good angel, Mr. Valcour."

Valcour felt stuffed, and was mad at the swift hot blush that seemed to escape from his collar and wash up over his face. He felt absurdly stupid as he said, "I would like to be." It was imperative to confer with Simpson and to have that essential talk with Slade, to force Slade to throw some light on the remarkable if obscure statement which he had sent by letter to the commissioner, and a copy of which Valcour had in his pocket. His eyes had been carefully taking in the room. Nothing was disarranged in it at all, and nothing seemed out of place. "I shan't disturb you any further, Mrs. Willett, for the present." He signaled Simpson with his eye to meet him just as soon as she could leave the room, and then he went out in the wide, spacious hallway, with its open well for the stairs that led to the floors above, and to the one below. The lighting in the hall was bad. It came filtered through a skylight set in the roof above the stair well. He recognized a figure approaching him as Detective Blaine who was acting, at the moment, as a footman.

"Where's Slade?" Valcour said.

"He's probably up in his room, Lieutenant. Shall I get him?"

"Yes. I'll see him down in the library. Where have you been for the past quarter of an hour, Blaine?"

"In the pantry and dining room, sir. Slade's had me polishing silver."

Valcour nodded toward Mrs. Willett's closed door. "What do you know about this?"

"Nothing."

"What did they do here this morning?"

Detective Blaine took out a small notebook. He thumbed it, and started to read: "'The car arrived at nine-fifty. Mrs. W. went immediately to her room. Young Mrs. W. went up to her own room, on the same floor as old Mrs. W.'s room, in the rear. Henry W. and W. Strange went to what is called the boys' room on the third floor back. Mrs. W. rang for Slade at ten-five. Mrs. W. went with Slade all over the house, including kitchen, servants' quarters, and basement. Young Mrs. W. and Henry W. both tried to leave house but were prevented by Jensen at front door, this at ten-fifteen. Jensen states young Henry W. kicked him on shin. Old Mrs. W. finished inspection of house and returned to her room at eleven. At eleven-five Slade set me at silver.'" Blaine closed the notebook. "Outside of that kick on the shin, Lieutenant, nothing unusual happened."

"Get Slade."

"Yes, sir."

Valcour went on down the broad oak stairs. It irritated him to realize that his nerves were jumpy. The case could and probably would be closed at once. Everything hinged on Slade. Slade would close it with a word, if there was any foundation at all to that pregnant statement which he had posted to the commissioner. What a curious and conflicting mess it was! Larry certainly did not use either rouge or a tinted face powder on his cheeks, and yet the state's attorney had been definitely (and quite rightly) unwilling to dismiss Larry entirely, and had only grudgingly admitted him to bond because of the strong and earnest personal request of the commissioner. Linda did use both rouge and a tinted face powder on her cheeks (and had admittedly handled that gun) but so did Mrs. Willett.

"You had best be looking out for yourself, Lieutenant, if you go back in there."

Valcour paused at the foot of the stairs and stared toward Jensen. "Why?" he said.

"That young hellion has just this minute been after going back there into the library. I couldn't swear to it, but I'm thinking he stuck his tongue out at me."

"Is he alone?"

"Yes, Lieutenant." Jensen added bitterly: "That's all he needs to be."

The library had a gold-leafed ceiling, book-lined walls, and massive Italian furniture. Henry was lolling on a scarlet velvet throne chair before a log fire that burned on a black marble hearth. He was reading, with intensive concentration, an unexpurgated edition of the *Thousand-and-One Nights*. "Ah, there, Valcour," he said, "listen to this. This is hot." He read several passages out loud. "What do you think of that?" Valcour stood on the hearth and stared down at Henry's uncouth features and disordered hair. He smiled faintly and said, "You mustn't kick my men on the shins."

Henry was buried in the book. "Oh, that," he said.

"You're liable to go to jail if you do."

"The beast wouldn't let me go to the movies."

After a minute Valcour said, "Did you know that your mother fell down and hurt herself?"

Henry stared at him stupidly, and then looked again at the book. "You're interrupting me. I wish you'd go away," he said.

Valcour's voice was very gentle. "Why did you put that twenty thousand dollars in Larry's trunk?"

The book slid and flopped onto the floor and Henry said sharply, "I didn't."

"I think you did. Don't you like Larry?"

Henry shouted at the top of his lungs, "I didn't put it in his trunk." His eyes were sly-looking, and he added more quietly, "But I know who did." He picked the book up from the floor. "You made me lose my place, you beast."

"Who did put it there, then?"

"Larry."

"Oh, come now. I bet you don't know after all."

Henry's face was reddening with anger. He started to shout again. "He did too. Larry put it there himself. I saw Larry put it there himself."

"When?"

"The day we left the beastly camp. His pockets were stuffed with money and he put it in his trunk. He's a thief." He had found his place in the book and was at once absorbed in it. Valcour fell a fleeting kinship to Hamlet—to believe or not to believe—and Henry's fingers were twisting hair, and knotting hair, and yanking it flat again. Then Blaine came in and said: "Slade isn't in his room, Lieutenant."

"Look through the house."

"I have."

"He's gone out?"

"Must have, sir."

"You've questioned Jensen?"

"Yes, and no one has gone out by the front door."

"How about the servants' entrance?"

"Patrolman Harris has been sitting by it all morning. No one has used it."

"The back yard?"

"High walls, and scarcely scalable, sir, and the door opening onto the roof is bolted on the inside."

"Then unless the roof door was bolted by somebody after he left, Slade is still in the house."

"Would you two mind going out in the hall and doing your talking?" Henry said mildly. "I am reading a book."

Blaine's fingers were itching, and even Valcour's contracted a little. "Been through all the rooms?" he said.

"All the unoccupied ones, sir."

"Then come with me while we inquire at the occupied ones."

"Good-bye, beasties," said Henry.

"If I could but once lay the print of my five fingers on—"

"Come, come, Blaine," said Valcour.

They went up the broad oak stairs and past the door to Mrs. Willett's room. "Simpson's in with her," Valcour said. "What's that door there?"

"It's a linen closet, Lieutenant."

"Open it."

Blaine tried the handle. "It's locked."

"Who would have the key?"

"Slade."

"Whereupon we say, in regard to the linen closet, Keno. Do you know what Keno means?"

"No, Lieutenant."

"Neither do I. Whose door is this?"

"Jess Willett and his wife's room."

Valcour knocked, and Linda's voice said, "Yes? Who is it?"

"Lieutenant Valcour. Is Slade in there, please?"

The door remained shut. "Slade? Why, no, Mr. Valcour."

"Have you seen him recently?"

"Why, no—not for an hour or more."

"Thank you." They moved along the hall. "How about these doors, Blaine?"

"All empties, Lieutenant. What a waste! Think of the tenements, Lieutenant. Stuffed."

"I don't want to think of the tenements. Besides, when you get to be rich you'll find out that the hallmark lies in having a lot of things that you don't use."

Slade was not with Wilbur in the boys' room upstairs, nor in Larry's room, nor in any servant's room, and Valcour and Blaine were down on the second floor again, and Valcour said suddenly: "Give me your flashlight."

He took the flashlight and played it steadily on the linen locker door. "That little smear?"

"Yes, Blaine. I thought it was, and now I'm sure of it. It's blood."

CHAPTER 27

"If you think it wise, madam."

Simpson began arranging things for Mrs. Willett, who was in the process of getting up. The corsets fascinated Simpson. It had been years since she had stifled her stomach, as a girl, in a pair of them. But you never could tell, what with the new styles and everything. She caught herself wishing that she could try them on. Maybe they'd give her hips. She needed hips.

"I think it will be quite safe, Simpson. My head is much better."

"I'm glad of that, madam. Shall I have your trunks sent up, and unpack? I dare say they may be here by now. The delivery is pretty quick from the docks."

"Later. I'll wear the dress I wore off the boat for the present." She walked to a dresser and stared in its mirror at her face. That couldn't be her face. She said quite suddenly, "You are a policewoman, Simpson, are you not?"

Simpson stopped dead in the middle of her arrangings. "Yes, Mrs. Willett."

"I thought so. You are not the caliber of the true domestic. You are here because—?" Mrs. Willett put on a dressing gown and headed for the bathroom. She left the question hanging delicately in the air.

"Because the commissioner thought it advisable, madam."

"Of course. He is kind. He is very kind. He is one of the kindest men, Simpson, I have ever known."

Simpson put a cambric chemise down on a chair and faced Mrs. Willett. "He is genuinely solicitous about you, madam. About your general safety." She said with a flat earnestness: "A great many people don't understand him. He's such a gentleman. He's a real gentleman."

"He should be," Mrs. Willett said. "He was born one."

She went into the bathroom and closed its door, and Simpson with puzzled and efficient eyes went quickly to the bed. She lay down on it. She sat up on its edge. She stood up and tried to tangle her feet in the rug along its side. She couldn't. It would have taken a contortionist, she decided, to get out of that bed, trip, and bang her head on the foot of the bed. Mrs. Willett wasn't a contortionist. She was simply a badly frightened old woman who was not telling the truth. Why? What had given her that blow on the head? Who had given it to her? Why was she shielding her attacker, if there had been an attacker? For love? Simpson shrugged. It certainly was a crime what limits some women would go to for love. And, she added bitterly (with half of her mind on an expert peterman whom she had once tried to reform), for what?

"Simpson," came from behind the bathroom door.

"Yes, Mrs. Willett?"

"Will you be good enough to get me a cup of boiling water?"

"Certainly, madam."

"Thank you."

Simpson went out and closed the door. She saw the bright shaft of Valcour's flashlight playing on the linen locker door. She heard him say to Blaine: "It's blood."

Her own blood congealed in cold knots. Her work on the force lay in larceny cases, not homicide. And that's what blood was—wasn't it?—homicide. She leaned back against Mrs. Willett's door and hoped that she wasn't going to make a show of herself and faint. Valcour saw her and said: "Where would there be a key to this door?"

She managed to walk over to them and say, "Slade has the keys for all rooms in the house, Lieutenant."

"No duplicates?"

"None that I know of."

Valcour examined the door. It was good solid oak, and the lock looked strong. He said to Blaine, "Go down in the cellar and see if you can get an axe."

Blaine was off on a run, and Simpson knew that her cheeks were covered with a cold sweat. "Someone is dead in back of there, Lieutenant?"

"We shall see. What reports have you?"

"Just that bruise on Mrs. Willett's head. I don't believe her story."

"Neither do I. Any idea how it happened?"

"No Lieutenant. I tried it out, the way she said she got it, and it isn't possible. You couldn't possibly get out of that bed, and trip, and hit your head on its foot." She could see the little smear now. It was very red.

"How did you find her? Hear anything? Hear her fall?"

"No, I didn't hear anything. I was bringing up a tray for her. Some tea and toast. She didn't answer my knock, so I went in. She was lying on the floor and I picked her up and put her on the bed."

"Whereabouts on the floor?"

"Just alongside of the bed, Lieutenant." Those running steps on the stairs. That would be Blaine with an axe.

"Was she unconscious?"

"Yes."

"Did you revive her before coming downstairs?"

"Yes, Lieutenant. There were some spirits of ammonia in the medicine locker of the bathroom. I gave her some after having brought her to with smelling salts." It was Blaine. He was running toward them along the hall. In his hand was an axe.

"What was the first thing she said?"

"She said, 'Not yet,' Lieutenant."

"Sure of it?—Just a minute, Blaine."

"Yes. It was a funny thing to say."

"Did she explain it at all?"

"No."

"You questioned her?"

"I didn't have to, Lieutenant. She told me what had happened. Then she started to look faint again. She looked terrible. It frightened me, and I ran downstairs to get help. You had just come in with Mr. Willett and Mr. Stone." Blaine was hefting the axe.

"All right. Go in to her now and keep her in her room until we find out what's behind this door. Don't let her come out into the hall."

"No, Lieutenant."

Simpson was gone into Mrs. Willett's room, and Valcour said to Blaine: "Split that panel."

Steel crashed on wood and a jagged gap widened. Valcour pushed a flashlight through the rough opening that the axe had made, and pressed its switch. A door had opened down the hall, and footsteps were running on the stairs. Blaine said sharply to Jess and Larry and Linda and Wilbur Strange, "Keep back—just a minute, people—keep back."

Valcour turned to him. "Call up headquarters and get the crew up here."

"Slade, sir?"

"Yes. I think it's unquestionably a suicide. The key is on the inside of the door. There's a bullet hole in his head."

CHAPTER 28

The commissioner of the New York police force held Mrs. Willett's hand until she withdrew it. It wasn't Kate's hand, not a bit, this chill and knobby thing of bone and flesh, and no effort of his mind could transmute it into the strong and capable little hand that he had known, those years ago, as little Kate's.

"You will forgive me for receiving you in here, John. There is that terrifying formality in the rooms downstairs that is still too unaccustomed from disuse to make them habitable."

She led him past the huge mahogany bed and toward two deep and comfortable armchairs by a window. It was the farthest point in the room from that closed door from behind whose panels came faint voices, the intermittent passage of many feet, stillnesses, and then sounds again, all commingling into a strangeness that was, she knew, the several branches of the law at work upon their different duties. Upon (the fact rushed at her with horrible clarity) Slade's suicide.

The commissioner looked at her obliquely. What an aging there had been! Scarcely two weeks, wasn't it, he wondered, since he had been looking at her from across a bowl of pale fresh roses on the desk down in his office? Dissolution. There was something nasty about the word and he changed it rather to a melting. Certain very definite things had simply melted inside of her and left her skin without its proper support. He said: "We must talk frankly, Kate."

Her over-large eyes left the broad tree-fringed walk that bordered the park, left the two knob-kneed youngsters who were tricycling in circles about their plump and much starched nursemaid, (why was there ever any growth in little children—wasn't heaven simply a nursemaided park reserved in blessed lovingness for little children?) and rested—those eyes—on the virile and kind features of the man so near to her on that chair. "Yes, John," she said.

"What's at the bottom of all this—really at the bottom of it?"

"I don't think I know what you mean."

"I mean this: is it money? Hate? Jealousy? Revenge? What has motivated all these things—the threat notes, the twenty thousand dollars hidden in Larry's trunk, Arthur's death, and now Slade's suicide?"

Mrs. Willett started and paled sharply at a booming crack that came from behind the closed hall door. "That," said the commissioner, "is a flashlight. I should have warned you that they'd take them. They're making pictures of the linen closet. There will be others."

"Pictures?"

"Yes. Of Slade. Different things. They're taking no chances."

"I see." Her lips were still pallid.

"Well, Kate, what about it?"

She said very simply, "I shan't lie to you. I don't think that I could lie to you, John. I shall say nothing."

He stared at the firm closed line of those dreadful and pale lips. Little Kate had closed her lips like that. She had closed them like the time the grocer's delivery boy at Tuxedo had set fire to the stables from a carelessly dropped cornsilk cigarette and she had been placed in a bad light about it. From nine to nine and a half years of age she had been violently in love with that grocer boy's hypnotic ability to stand for a record stretch of two full minutes on his head. The commissioner wondered irrelevantly what head-standings there had been to have fascinated her into that unfathomable marriage with Allenby Mortimer Willett. "You're putting me in an uncomfortably embarrassing position, Kate," he said.

"In what way, John?"

"In every way. Who's your grocer boy this time?"

The question confused her. It sank gently into the maelstrom of her mind, whirled languidly down to the bottom, and was thrown out again.

"Grocer?"

"You remember that time at Tuxedo—the grocer boy—the stable fire. He stood on his head."

Fifty years of veiling were torn to shreds and very clearly she could see it. But she wasn't seeing it (that was the curious part of it), she was being it—the smell of hay soft in the vast cool stable—the head-standings—the dropped cigarette—smoke curling upwards softly—higher, blacker—screams and rushing men and pails and pails of water that had saved the stables—and that agonizing sweetness of her mother's voice: "Thank God—God, I thank Thee"—snatching her to her...the calm wide eyes beneath a large black pompadour dazed with relief and shock and fright...

"Biff."

"That's right, Kate. His name was Biff." The commissioner added gently, "What is it this time?"

"There isn't any Biff, John," she said.

She could sense the formalness coming suddenly into him, watched apathetically their momentary unity receding like a wave and leaving cold gray stretches of blank sands unmarked by any footprints. She did not wish to step out across those sands even if, at their retreating edge, she would find, if she hurried, a meeting-up with him again.

"As you wish, Kate."

He felt deeply and badly hurt, the more so at his unreasonably growing anger than at anything else. He could see perfectly well that she had her side. After all, when you came right down to it, he was the Police Commissioner of New York City and Kate was a woman about whom revolved odd deaths and events and who indubitably held some important knowledge connected with their cause. Her pigtails were at him through those moist and tired old eyes. And here he was, badgering her. It was what it amounted to. Sticking a probe into the private places of her heart, and her heart would surely be all that was left of her (the melting process seemed to be going on even while he was watching) if she didn't soon find some sort of release. He damned the whole thing. She mustn't keep them, those private places. Even if they were all she had left out of a lifetime—and heaven knew it wasn't much to have as salvage—and no matter what it was she had stored up in them she mustn't, for her own sake, keep them. He stood up.

"Don't hurry, John."

"Good God, Kate! Hurry?" He stared at her wincing under the sudden and explosive force of his voice. "Are you mad? Do suicide and danger and murder mean nothing to you at all? Is there no significance in the fact that there is a murderer near you, sheltered by you, probably cherished by you, living in this house?"

"Stop, John—I beg you stop—"

"I won't stop. You must wake up. You must be shaken from this stupid lethargy—this resignation—this—Dear God, Kate, what is it?"

She cried, it seemed to her, so easily these days and so very much. It was funny to have spent a lifetime without any tears and then to have so many of them within two little weeks. How quiet and clear and spacious tears made your head feel! "Allenby, my love," she said, "you mustn't talk so loudly. You will strain your throat."

He felt as if a club had hit him on the head. He was down on his knees before her, staring sharply into her dull, moist eyes. "You know me, don't you, little Kate?"

"Of course, dear Allenby. How dark your hair looks in this light."

"Kate—Kate!"

"John? Yes, John? Why are you down there on your knees?"

He got to his feet, and his manner was nervously apologetic. She would forgive him if he went. Later—they would talk again later. Either that evening, or to-morrow. Just now there were so many things to do.

She had no conception of the intricacies and all but overwhelming details forced upon him by his office. She was not to worry. Not one bit. Her fingers were bloodless flesh and her eyes two small balloons drifting off to nothingness through distant mists, and he closed the door and walked past cluttering tripoded cameras, past two men crouched by the linen closet, past a parchment and unearthly face with a bullet hole dead in the center of its forehead, and down oak stairs to Valcour.

He said to him rapidly: "Have Simpson found, please. Tell her to stay with Mrs. Willett and not to leave her. I am going to Stiernheim. He is the best psychiatrist in the city. I will arrange either to bring him here myself or to have him call on Mrs. Willett some time to-day. See that he sees her, and that her family does not interfere." He added distinctly, "See that neither of her sons can interfere."

"She told you something of importance, Commissioner?"

"Valcour, she puzzles me. There is something frightening about her. I believe she knows. I do not dare press her further until we have an opinion by Stiernheim. There was one moment when she called me by her husband's name. It was like a blow on the head. You are in complete charge here. If you want to, you can fill this house with men and keep a guard on every person connected with it until this case is solved."

CHAPTER 29

It is a commonplace to speak about the lull before a storm. Everyone has experienced it: that muffled, electric tension, so charged with menace, which is a thick dark hood drawn over the head, making invisible the dreadful forces that are straining, and that will with the shock of an anticipated suddenness so violently slip their leash.

Valcour had felt it closing about him as the commissioner left the house. More obscurely it pressed all about him during the few hours in which the customary routine connected with a death by violence was efficiently gone through by the various details from headquarters, by men from the medical examiner's office and the district attorney's office. At four o'clock it hung in the house like intangible shade when the men had gone and Slade's body had been removed to an undertaking establishment.

The gun had been found on the cupboard floor beside him. The medical examiner had officially pronounced him a suicide.

The house was a prison. A man was posted on each of its four floors, and one in the basement to guard the rear door into the yard, in addition to the man in the basement's front at the servants' entrance. Mrs. Willett was in her room, resting, with cool cloths kept on her head by Simpson, who never left her.

It was shaded and quiet in the long narrow drawing room on the ground floor, and Linda's features were not very clear in the depths of the chair where she sat. Valcour drew his own a little nearer. "You will tell me, please," he said, "why you intended to kill your husband."

A filigree gilt clock on the mantel-shelf ticked and ticked and Linda caught each one of them as a hammer tap inside her head. She said very evenly, "It is Slade who is dead."

"Slade is a suicide. He is a stepping stone."

She was nervously alert and said, "From what to what, Mr. Valcour?"

He shrugged. "Slade killed himself because he thought he knew who murdered Arthur. It was his intention to disclose that knowledge to the police. He found, at the last minute, that he could not."

"Because he was wrong?"

"Because," Valcour said, "he was right. I am as positive of that as if he had told me so. I wish that he had told me so. His knowledge died with him." He repeated, "Why did you intend to kill your husband?"

"Are you connecting me with the cause of Slade's suicide?"

"I am ignoring Slade. The starting point is back in camp with Arthur's death. You were about to tell me what you really did with that gun, which you found on the morning of the day that Arthur was murdered in a corner of the camp's living room, when we were interrupted by your husband that night on board the *Hamilton*. Tell me now."

Linda wondered why pressing her fingers down hard on the arms of the chair didn't stop them from trembling. She said quite suddenly, "Do you know what a snob is?"

Valcour smiled. "Well, yes. Don't I?"

"I don't think you do. If you did, there wouldn't be any question in your mind about it. It's one of the things you either know or don't. I know. I married one." It was an effort for her to add: "I love one."

It was bewildering. "Suppose he is? You wouldn't want to kill him for that."

"Does anyone ever want to kill anyone just for one definite thing?"

"No, I suppose they don't. There are usually contributory causes. But there's always a main cause. You aren't advancing snobbery, are you, as yours?"

"Aren't you taking an admission of my intention rather for granted, Mr. Valcour?"

"Not really. You yourself have been pointedly secretive and confusing as to your whole connection with that gun. Your statements to Slade on the morning of the day of the murder were quite significant. Shall I recall them to you? You said that the bullet of that gun was too small to hurt, and that the sound of it was too gentle to hear. You stated under oath at the inquest that you had taken that gun into your room, and refused to explain why you had done so. On the boat you said to me that you had lied. You did not take that gun into your room. Where did you take it?"

Her throat was getting dry and thick. She said: "It was taken from me."

"By whom?"

"I don't know."

He stared at the frightened eyes in her pale still face. He observed the dreadful nervousness of her hands. "You must tell me just what happened," he said.

"Do you remember that hallway up at camp, Mr. Valcour, which runs through the sleeping quarters?"

"Yes."

"There's no window in it."

"Well?"

"Only when some of the doors are open is there any light in it. Even when the door from the living room is open it is hard to see in it."

"Yes?"

"I left the living room with the gun. I started down that hall. There is a door to the kitchen on the left. It opened and someone took the gun from me and gave me a shove. I hurt my shoulder on the opposite wall. That's all there is to it, Mr. Valcour."

He said quietly, "I don't think so. You recognized the person who gave you that shove."

"I didn't."

"You recognized something about the person who gave you that shove."

She said: "Hair." It was a mumble, really.

"I beg your pardon?"

"Just hair, Mr. Valcour. It might have been Arthur or Henry."

"Or your husband."

"It couldn't have been." She was very sure of that. Whatever else Jess might have done, he never would have done that. "He'd never have pushed me. He's never pushed me—done anything like that."

The picture was wrong. It was crazy. One didn't dash out of a kitchen door, snatch a gun away from a woman walking through a hall, and give her a push that sent her hard against the opposite wall. Valcour couldn't visualize Jess or Larry or Wilbur doing a thing like that. He couldn't even visualize Arthur or Henry doing it...or Slade... "What were you doing?" he said suddenly.

The question startled her. Her eyes were frightened-looking. "Nothing. Just walking. Just walking along the hallway, Mr. Valcour, with the gun."

He could see obstinacy hardening in her, a crystallizing determination to conceal whatever had been her true purpose in regard to that gun. He said: "You have called your husband a snob. I am stupid about it. Just what did you mean?"

The city was alive about them, its sounds diluted through the drawing room's front windows—motors—heavy buses—the general, faint, distinctive blend. "One must remember his background," she said.

"His bringing up?"

Her eyes were speculative. "I suppose that is it, rather. His bringing up." She named a prep school that was well known for the rigidity of its exclusiveness and said, "Willett sons are automatically born into it."

"But isn't all that more or less of a different age? With four-in-hands and cotillions?"

"The Willetts have remained of a different age."

She was so singularly impersonal about it. There was no identifying of herself with the Willett family at all. She was off somewhere, watching her body in its state of being married in the Willett family, but she wasn't in it herself.

"And aren't such things relative?" Valcour said.

"Quite. My own family is perfectly good country stock. We've had a lieutenant governor and a judge. We've also taken in boarders." She added as a plain statement of fact, "Jess is ashamed that we have taken in boarders."

And again what of it? Add to the fact of your husband being a snob his additional distaste for the business of taking in boarders and still you wouldn't normally want to kill him for it. He smiled amiably and said, "He keeps referring to it?"

"Unfortunately, he doesn't."

That, to a measure, was understandable. Unspoken things, when you are aware of their existence, do fester. "You have thought of leaving him?" he said. It was so much simpler than murder. But people who were emotionally pressed were seldom simple in their choice of a way out.

She said: "Mr. Valcour, I've told you once that I'm not clever. I've no aptitude for explaining things. I loved Jess more than anything on earth. He was all I could think about. I'd go to bed thinking about him, and when I woke up I was still thinking about him. When he wasn't with me I wasn't living. I married him. I love him still. I've wanted to kill him. I've wanted to leave him. I've wanted to kill myself." She shrugged. "I've done none of those things. I never will."

A patrolman was fidgeting on one foot by the door. "Well?" Valcour said to him.

"A Dr. Stiernheim, Lieutenant. He's in the hall."

"I will be right there."

"Yes, sir."

Valcour stood up. He looked at Linda. He said casually, "By the way, do you happen to use Alberta Marlboro face powder and rouge?"

"Why, yes—I do."

CHAPTER 30

Simpson went on with the unpacking of Mrs. Willett's trunks. They had been brought up and were standing in the bedroom. There were two. One of them was already emptied and the other one almost so. Simpson decided that a good many of the things that she came across in them were a caution. She knew that Mrs. Willett, in her arm-chair by the window, wasn't reading. She hadn't turned a leaf of that book in her hands for more than five minutes. Riches, Simpson decided, while placing the last of the cambric chemises in a drawer, weren't everything. Not by a jugful. One look at that drawn and tired old face was enough to prove that. She answered a knock on the door, and let a maid in with a tray containing buttered toast and tea. She set a table before Mrs. Willett and had the tray placed on it. She arranged with the maid to have the trunks sent up for shortly, and closed the door.

"Would you be good enough to send for my son Henry?"

"Yes, Mrs. Willett."

Simpson opened the door to call the maid, but she had already gone. There was no one in the hall but the plainclothes-man on guard, sitting on a chair by the stair well, staring at a painting of the seashore (with a boat on an even keel on the sands and its stern facing inland) and wondering how it got that way.

"You will probably find him in his room, on the floor above in the rear," Mrs. Willett said.

"Yes, madam."

Simpson wasn't sure what she ought to do. It would take only a minute, of course, to run upstairs and get Henry, and if she left the room door open that guard by the stair well could see right into the room… one didn't execute orders with absolute literalness…there was always a latitude allowed within reason…she hurried to the stairs and ran up them, along the upper hall to the rear, and knocked on a door. It opened almost at once, and Henry looked out at her.

"Your mother would like to see you. She is in her room."

Henry negligently took in Simpson from her head to her shoes. "Oh, all right," he said. "I bet you never stopped any traffic."

Simpson compressed her lips. She hurried back along the hall and down the stairs and into the room again. Mrs. Willett was still sitting in her armchair at the window by the tea table, with her book. But it wasn't the same book. An inexplicable chill ran along Simpson's prominent spine as she realized it. She was certain that the book which Mrs. Willett had had in her hand when she had gone upstairs had had a bright yellow jacket. The jacket on this one was blue. It didn't mean anything, really—she convinced herself of this—simply that during her short absence, Mrs. Willett must have got up from her chair, taken another book, and then sat down again. She was getting nerves, that's what it was, and it wasn't very often, when out on a case, that Simpson got nerves.

"Did you tell him?" Mrs. Willett said.

"Yes, madam."

"Thank you."

The last of the things were out of the trunks and Simpson closed them up.

"Are you staying in here on purpose?"

"The commissioner thought it advisable if someone were in the room with you, Mrs. Willett. I hope that it won't disturb you too much."

"It doesn't disturb me at all. I appreciate his thoughtfulness." She looked directly at the younger woman. "When you get to be as old as I am, Simpson, you will find that thoughtfulness is a rather priceless thing."

There it was again, Simpson decided—the curse-of wealth. There wasn't a thing in this world that that old woman in the chair couldn't buy if she wanted to—clothes, jewels, travel, amusement—anything, everything—and yet there she sat. Blighted. Simpson had been in the country on a case late one fall. One night the dahlias in a garden were blighted by frost. And that was the way Mrs. Willett looked now.

Mrs. Willett tentatively felt the teapot and a silver hot-water jug. She fumbled around in a large handbag on her lap and took out a small bottle of tablets. "Saccharine," she said. "I am not permitted sugar." She tried the cap and then held the bottle toward Simpson. "Would you see if you can unscrew this for me, please? Jess ordered them this afternoon. I have difficulty in loosening the top of each new bottle."

Simpson unscrewed the cap and placed the bottle on the tea table, and Henry came into the room and closed the door and walked over and sat down in the armchair beside Mrs. Willett's.

"I will have lemon in it to-day," he said.

It was a singular and regular process, this afternoon teaing on the part of Henry and Mrs. Willett. Its mechanics were thoroughly understood by both of them. Arthur had been a party to them too, before his death. Now there was just Henry. He would be reasonably polite, sufficiently mannered while he drank his tea, as talkative as he pleased, and after its brief quarter of an hour was over he would collect five dollars. "You're a fool, Kate," Larry had said to her several years ago about it. She had shrugged and said, "You buy seats for a play. You know it is illusion. But it gives you at least a visual picture of what might have been." She had never forgot Larry's answer that the portrait of a hamburg steak had never as yet kept a hungry man from starving.

Simpson effaced herself discreetly in a corner and sorted stockings and soiled linen for the laundry, and Mrs. Willett looked at the attempted slicking down of Henry's hair and said, "How many lumps will it be this afternoon, dear boy?"

"Three, if you please, Mother dear."

Five dollars.

Henry stared through the window at the motors swinging southward on the avenue below. He wondered whether he could slip past that beast down by the front door and take his own car out for a spin that night. He could shake Wilbur, sneak out, and go on up along the Concourse. Sometimes you could pick up a girl along the Concourse. Why stop at the Concourse? Why not get right out of the city until this business was over? The camp? The avenue lamps turned suddenly on were pale pools in twilight.

"It's dark in this room," he said.

"It is very restful. My eyes arc tired, dear boy."

"Just as you wish it, Mother."

Five dollars.

He stirred the sugar in his cup and, with an over-excess of delicacy, sipped hot tea. Bellywash. Of all the bellywash. There was a bottle of whiskey hidden in a drawer in his room. He'd take some of that along, if he got out to-night.

"What are you thinking of, child?"

Mrs. Willett also sipped her tea, and Simpson over in her distant corner felt that if a light weren't turned on soon she'd blind herself. The stockings in the dimness were all of one color.

"Of nothing, Mother."

"You are fortunate, if that is true." How soft and young his features looked in twilight! There was a touch of Allenby about them. Dear Allenby. How intimately fond and selective was remembrance! Like twilight it softened every harsh and ugly thing. It had softened Allenby to her into a comfortable (and certainly strange) rosiness. The best of him was all there, in strange rosiness.

Henry set down his cup. He diddled after small talk, and said, "Very nice, I'm sure."

"A little more?"

"No, thank you."

She fumbled in her bag, then put her hand in his coat pocket as he bent to complete their bargain with a kiss. She said, "I've put it in your pocket." She kissed him back, and he felt a prick of annoyance at this innovation in the routine. She followed his figure through the room's pale darkness, and then she finished her tea.

"Shall I turn on a lamp, madam?"

"Not yet for a while, Simpson." Mrs. Willett stood up and walked over to the bed. "I shall lie down and rest."

Simpson moved, with her stockings, to the vacated chair by the window and went on with them there. A quarter of an hour passed before she had finished them. Then she sat quite still, after the sorting was done, and stared down at the park, at the purple shadows deep beneath trees in twilight, until a quiet rap on the door brought her to her feet. She went over and opened it.

"Yes, Lieutenant."

"Mrs. Willett?"

"She is resting."

"I am afraid that we will have to wake her." Valcour indicated the solidly built, immaculately dressed, brusque man beside him. "This is Dr. Stiernheim. He is to see Mrs. Willett."

Dr. Stiernheim eyed the room's shadows with disfavor. "A light, if you please," he said.

Simpson pressed a switch and the six-bracketed ormolu chandelier flared garishly. Dr. Stiernheim headed at once for the bed. They heard the sharp hiss of his breath. "This woman," he said, "is dead."

CHAPTER 31

Dr. Stiernheim was being curtly technical: "The heart has been arrested in diastole. There has been a paralytic action on the respiratory center. You will note, please, the dilation of the pupils, and what one would presume to be symptoms of asphyxiation." He turned to Simpson and said: "What has this woman been drinking?"

"Tea." Simpson felt wretched. The cold little beads were breaking out on her face again. She pointed to the tea table, to the empty cups.

Dr. Stiernheim crossed to the table, sniffed Henry's cup, put it down, sniffed Mrs. Willett's and touched his tongue to the dregs. "As I thought," he said. "She has been poisoned by an overdose of tincture of aconite. Less than a spoonful would have been enough to be fatal. You will find, Lieutenant, that the autopsy will prove my contention to be correct, and if you will permit me to I will run along. I am a busy man. There is nothing that I can do here. Advise me, please, if I am later required for any formalities."

"There is just one thing, Doctor." Valcour stopped him at the door. "Is the taste of aconite noticeable?"

"Noticeable, yes, but not unpleasant. It is possible that taken in strong tea, as this was, and especially if this woman's mind were overwrought, the flavor of the drug would not be noticed. You will forgive me? I shall bid you good-day."

"Doctor—if you please, one moment. Doctor."

"Well?"

Simpson went to him at the door and handed him the small glass bottle. "Mrs. Willett said that these are saccharine. She put some in her tea. Are they?"

Dr. Stiernheim unscrewed the cap and touched his tongue to one of the white pellets. "Just so," he said. "They are saccharine." He handed back the bottle.

"Then they aren't aconite?"

"The aconite which this woman took, my good woman, was in liquid form. Good-day to you, good-day, sir. Good-day." The door closed with a competent bang.

"Tell me at once," Valcour said, "what happened here." Simpson recounted her corner-version of the tea party. "There was one thing that did strike me as odd, Lieutenant."

"Yes?"

"When I left Mrs. Willett to go upstairs to get Henry, she had a book in her hand. When I came down again—it couldn't have been longer than three minutes—she was sitting right in the same spot, but she had a different book in her hand."

Valcour's eyes narrowed a little. "What made you notice it?"

"I couldn't help noticing it, Lieutenant. The one she had in her hand when I went upstairs had a bright yellow jacket, and when I came back it was blue."

"Why did you go upstairs to get Henry?"

"Mrs. Willett sent me."

"Do you know what she wanted him for?"

"To take tea with her, I imagine. He did."

"He sat here and drank tea?"

"Yes, Lieutenant."

"Any row?"

"Row? Oh, no, he seemed very quiet and well-behaved." There was food for thought. "Did you watch him?"

"While they were having tea?"

"Yes."

"I did glance over occasionally. He seemed to be just sitting there, sipping tea. The room was quite dark."

"Did they talk?"

"Just a few words. Nothing significant at all."

"You noticed no motions that were odd?"

"No, Lieutenant. He just sat there. There *was* something, though."

"Well?"

"When he got up to go he leaned over and kissed Mrs. Willett, and I saw that she had her hand in his coat pocket. I think she said, 'I've put it in your pocket.'"

"Did you see what it was that she put in his pocket?"

"No, Lieutenant. Just her hand in it. That was all."

"Anything else to report?"

"No, Lieutenant."

"Then go down and telephone a report of this to headquarters. Please tell the man stationed upstairs on Henry's floor to see that Henry is in his room, and tell him to keep him there until I come. I have some work to do here."

"Yes, Lieutenant."

Simpson went outside and closed the door.

Valcour's heart was lead. The whole fabric of a definite theory which he had built up about the case collapsed with Mrs. Willett's death. He experienced an enervating listlessness of failure. Do? Jail the whole lot of them, was about all they could do. He smiled grimly. What was left of them. Linda and Jess and Larry and Henry and Wilbur Strange.

The aconite was in liquid form. Mrs. Willett had changed books. Mrs. Willett had used a new bottle of saccharine tablets ordered that afternoon for her by Jess. Suppose that the tablet which Dr. Stiernheim had tasted had been saccharine. There was nothing to prove that the tablets which Mrs. Willett had used in her tea, and which had lain on top, had been saccharine. But the aconite had been in liquid form. Unless Dr. Stiernheim, with his brusque and repellent manner, were fallible.

Valcour searched the room minutely. It was filled with Mrs. Willett. He could not keep his mind from her. She wasn't stiff and dead there on the bed. She was talking to him again from her beach chair down on the sands at Bermuda: "The early years don't matter, Mr. Valcour. There is a chance for change. It is the ending years that are so terrible. When things are set. When there is no hope or time left for changing. Things are accentuated in them too keenly. There is a sardonic sharpness in the absolute futility of their pain."

He emptied her handbag out onto the tea table. He recognized it as the same brocaded bag which she had carried with her in the grill room of the Hamilton, on the night of that wretched dancing fiasco of Linda and Henry and Wilbur. Its contents were a heterogeneous jumble—compact, loose bills, silver, a hair net, lip stick, a snapshot of Henry and Arthur taken at an age when complete nudity was a prerogative, a gold locket a crumpled piece of paper. He opened the locket and stared at an impressive young gentleman's face in sideburns. It was vaguely familiar. He closed the locket up again and then put it in his pocket. No wonder it was familiar. It was the face (taken heaven knew how many years ago) of the commissioner.

He stared at the test of the things. He stared at the crumpled paper. He smoothed it out. He felt a sudden swift surge of shock. It was coming back to him again—they were fitting—all the fragmentary, curious, significant little pieces were fitting—he did not know that he was running to the door and pulling it open until he found Simpson on the other side of it.

"Henry—" she began.

"Yes? He is in his room?"

"No, Lieutenant. He can't be found. Neither he nor that young Mr. Strange can be found."

For a flash he stared at Simpson's placid throat and wanted to strangle her. He said quietly, "The house has been gone over?"

"Well, yes, Lieutenant. The man on each floor has done his floor."

"Cupboards—bathrooms—under beds?"

Her eyes were on stems. "I'm sure I couldn't say as to under beds."

"Go back and tell them to cover the ground again—everything—comb it."

"The occupied rooms, too?'

"Yes, yes."

Simpson went off, and Valcour was back in Mrs. Willett's room, hurrying to the tea table and carefully examining again one of the objects from her handbag. He went into the connecting bathroom and turned on all its lights. Shelves, cabinets, hamper—nothing, nothing. The bathtub was ancient enough to be vintaged and wood paneling boxed it in from its curved metal rim to the floor. He got on his knees and opened the small door that masked the plumbing at the bath's end. He flashed his light inside. He whistled sharply and closed the door again. He was out of the bathroom, through the bedroom, and into the hall. The man on guard on that floor was coming toward him.

"Henry? Wilbur Strange?"

"Not a sign of them, sir."

"All right. Listen carefully to me, please. Take your chair and place it before the door to this room. You are to let no one in with the exception of the medical examiner and his assistants when they come. Ask him to touch nothing. Tell the other details from headquarters to keep out until I tell them otherwise."

"Yes, sir. Is it that this business is cleared up?"

"Cleared up? My dear man, we've got to move like hell or there'll be another murder."

CHAPTER 32

He said to Jess: "You will forgive me if I do not stop to express my sympathy appropriately—I see you have heard."

Jess was like a stunned rock standing in the hallway. Linda and Larry were two ghastly dummies on either side of him.

"A policeman told us, Mr. Valcour," Jess said.

"We can't go in to Kate? We must leave her in there all alone?" Larry's eyes had the incredulous and hurt look of a dog who cannot understand the reason for a whipping.

"Not yet, Mr. Stone," Valcour said. "Such things seem cruel. I must ask your forbearance. There is not a minute to lose."

Valcour ran up the stairs and back along the hall into the boys' room. Its lights were blazing and he stared for an instant, stunned, at Patrolman McBride's imitation of an ostrich.

"Pull your head out from under that bed, McBride. Anything there?"

"Now damn this bed," said McBride, rubbing the back of his skull where he'd cracked it at the sound of Valcour's voice. "There ain't a hide or hair of them on this whole floor, Lieutenant."

"When was the last time you saw them?"

"Come to think of it, I ain't seen the thick black one since he went into this room after lunch. That rough-haired blond pill went down soon after Simpson called him, that would be over half an hour ago."

"Did he come back up again?"

"He did. He was only gone down about ten minutes in all."

"Did you see him again?"

"I did not, Lieutenant. But I have my suspicions."

"Your what?"

Patrolman McBride, who was very earnest and very young, felt the back of his tall broad neck getting red. "I say that now I come to think of it, sir, I have my suspicions."

"Well, hurry up with them."

"The young scamp hadn't been in this room more than two minutes, or maybe three, when a phenomenon occurred down at that far end of the hall. The other end from this end, Lieutenant."

Valcour cast a suspicious sniff in the vicinity of McBride's earnest and snub nose, and said, "Don't ramble. What happened at the end of the hall?"

"Pops."

Valcour sniffed more deeply and again. "Pops?"

"Yes, sir. Pops. I went to investigate and found some peas at the bottom of the door. Maybe they was beans."

"Beanshooter?"

McBride's face was flaming. "Yes, sir. Beanshooter."

Valcour could see the business clearly: Henry distracting McBride's attention with the beanshooter, and then he and Wilbur Strange running down the service stairs that were at this end of the hall. Valcour left McBride and started running down the service stairs himself, to the door which opened from them into the entrance hallway on the ground floor. He said to the plainclothesman stationed there: "When did you last see Henry Willett and Wilbur Strange?"

"I haven't seen them at all since I've been on duty, Lieutenant. I don't know what they look like."

"Have you been in this hallway constantly?"

"Except just now since I've been looking through this floor for the two young men."

"You haven't left it at all except for that?"

"Well, there was that one minute, Lieutenant."

"What minute?" Valcour felt sick. More beanshooters? The tragic undercurrent of this silly freakishness, and its pressing menace, was thick in him.

"I heard a crash in the library and walked back to see what it was."

"What was it?"

"One of them jugs on the mantelpiece had fallen down and busted on the hearth. I looked around the library and there was nobody in it, and after that I looked all over this floor and it was empty, too, so I deduced it was a cat."

"What cat?"

"What else could it have been, Lieutenant?"

"You deduced that a house that had been closed for months, possibly for years, and that had only been opened up a few days would be likely to have a cat?"

"Why, one of the help might have brought one, Lieutenant."

Valcour shrugged and stared nervously at the front door. He could see Henry and Wilbur Strange walking calmly through it while its guard was investigating a smashed vase in the library. There were two exits from the library: one directly into the hallway and one opening into the drawing room. He pulled open the plate-glass iron-grilled door and stepped out into the vestibule and into the eager arms of six reporters.

"How long have you boys been here?" he said.

"For hours and hours and hours, Lieutenant, and if you'll just keep that death-clutch expression on your face for one more little min—" *Bang!* went the flashlight, turning the night, for a blinding second, whitish green.

Valcour said sharply, "Two young men came out of this door within the past hour. Any of you know where they went?"

"Rather." Mr. Montague Jones, of the city's most conservative paper, stroked a placid moustache. "They ambled toward the ancestral garage—a few blocks east, between Second and Third. We ambled with them."

"I can bet you did."

"He found our company depressing, the odd Willett one did. He seems to have a psychosis for shins."

"They went off in a car?"

"Went off is correct, Lieutenant. It was almost an explosion."

"Any inkling as to where they were headed for?"

"Well, when he wasn't calling us beasts there was the slight reference to a camp. Could that mean—"

The iron-grilled door slammed and Valcour was inside. He went upstairs and found Jess Willett. "What garage do you use for your cars?" he said. Jess told him. "Do you know their phone number?" Jess did.

Valcour went downstairs again and to a telephone. He called the garage. He checked the fact that Henry and Wilbur Strange had left there about fifty minutes ago in a high-powered roadster. The tank had been filled to capacity with gas. He jotted down the number of the license plates and a complete description of the car. Yes, the garage man had gathered that they were heading north. Something had been said about a camp. The crazy Willett boy was driving. He had scraped the garage door on the way out and had almost struck a pedestrian who was walking past on the street. The garage man hadn't filled the gas tank quite fast enough to suit, and that young Willett polecat had given him a kick on the…

Valcour slammed the receiver up, lifted it again, and was put through to headquarters. He gave the data for a general alarm and then hung up again. Soon, radiating from Centre Street, the great networked antennae of the New York police were reaching ever in widening circles from the city—north they went, information and instructions being given to the operator at each pause—Tarrytown, Poughkeepsie, Albany, and all places in between, and over on the west bank of the Hudson River the lines were flashing too…

A siren wailed out on Fifth Avenue—wailing and wailing, louder, louder—the peculiar individual and strident note which signified the commissioner's personal car. It might well have been the commissioner himself who was giving those dreadful cries, Valcour thought, as he put on his hat and coat and headed for the vestibule, and through reporters to the curb as the great limousine swung to a stop alongside.

Valcour got in at once and closed the door. He spoke rapidly and earnestly to the commissioner. The commissioner was impressed. The commissioner spoke to the driver and the car, with rising wails, shot north.

"The ferries—the Bear Mountain bridge, Valcour?"

"He would be too impatient for the ferries, Commissioner. And they would not as yet have had time to reach the bridge. Its approach, by now, is under guard."

CHAPTER 33

Henry giggled.

"You'd better not step on it so hard," Wilbur said. "There was a cop back there on that side road. I saw his motorcycle. Its lights were out." Wilbur's thick strong hands were clasped under the back of his neck. His legs were stretched and his heavy body was torpid upon deep leather cushions.

Henry giggled again and pressed the accelerator down to the floor. The speedometer needle swung gently from fifty to sixty-five—to eighty.

"You're crazy," Wilbur said indifferently, and the deep leather cushions were soft, as the night like a mad thing slithered by. Maybe the dead felt like this, Wilbur thought, when they were riding up to heaven. Side-guards on the windshield deflected the insane rush of cool night air from his face, and as he lay there with his head back there was nothing between his eyes and the bright wet stars. "Crossing the Bear Mountain bridge?"

"No," Henry said.

Far ahead on the road was a pinpoint of red. It wasn't the tail light of a car, because it was swinging in arcs—a fleck of bright scarlet red swinging in arcs. A lantern. Brakes gentled their hurtling down to forty-five and Henry turned suddenly to the right and roared along a road leading inland from the Hudson River, and into that maze of splendid cement byways that riddled Westchester County.

Henry held the car modestly at fifty. He wanted a drink. In the pocket of his coat was a small silver flask. He looked slyly at Wilbur, at Wilbur's strong and expressionless face held up, on clasped hands, to the stars. Wilbur didn't know about that flask. Henry giggled again. There were lots of things that Wilbur didn't know about.

The deep-bellied thrum of the powerful motor rushed by on the wind. They came to an intersecting road and he kept on straight ahead.

"You're taking us inland," Wilbur said.

"I know what I'm about."

"Not going to camp?"

"Yes, I'm going to the beastly camp."

"You don't like it there, do you?"

"No."

"Then why don't you turn back?"

"I don't want to."

Wilbur pushed deeper into leather. It didn't matter.

Henry's hand slid into his pocket and he felt the silver flask. Its top was screwed on pretty tight. He'd have to take both hands off the wheel in order to unscrew it. He took his hand out of his pocket. They'd stop somewhere along the road.

"Cop," said Wilbur.

"Isn't."

"It is."

"You're scared because I'm driving so fast."

"No, I'm not. Listen."

The staccato clatter of a motorcycle was strengthening in back of them. Henry slid the car up to eighty, down to fifty for a curve, suddenly braked her down to thirty, and swung her into the driveway of a private estate, where he killed the motor and shut off the lights. Like a rattle of drums the motorcycle grew louder and louder, roared at them, shot past, diminished—thinner—quite still.

Henry kicked the starter and backed out onto the road. He faced back along the route over which they had just come, and held it until, at a crossroad, he swung to the right.

"You're lost," Wilbur said.

"I'm not."

"You'll be fooling around these back roads here all night."

"I won't. That's the north star. We're going north."

Wilbur looked lazily. It was the north star. They were going north. "I'm going to telegraph your mother from Albany. I'm not going to have her worrying about you."

Henry said nothing to this. His face was crafty. He wanted a drink. "Isn't this fun?"

Wilbur turned his head and looked at Henry. He stretched his legs. He yawned a little. "Not bad," he said.

They saw a hamlet. They were through it. A shout, "Hey!" lingered in their ears, and a distant, indistinct "pop" that might have been a gun.

Henry giggled. "Hear that?"

"Yes, I heard it."

"That was a shot."

"They'll telephone ahead."

Henry was worried. "Think so?"

"They certainly will."

They swung to the left across a long bridge and about a mile farther on the concrete turned sharp to the right, while a dirt road continued on ahead. Henry held her onto the dirt road and brought her down to thirty as she plunged crazily in the ruts, through a great stretch of wooded darkness pierced by the car's wildly swinging white shafts of light.

"You'll ditch us," Wilbur said.

Henry didn't answer. He slowed her down to fifteen—to ten—then brought her to a complete stop on the grass-covered side of the road, switched off the engine, and turned off the lights.

"Shall we get out for a while, Wilbur?" he said politely.

"Suits me."

They were by the side of the road in the darkness. Crisp smells of fall leaves and shrubbery were pungent in the darkness. Henry started to move away. "It will be good to stretch a bit," he said.

Wilbur went with him. They walked along the soft dirt road—walked for minutes of silence along its tree-masked darkness, hearing acutely each of the lonely minor sounds that leaves and wind and branches make at night. Henry stopped abruptly, and his hand, in his coat pocket, started jiggling with the little silver flask.

"Want to turn back?"

"Yes, Wilbur, please," Henry said, "let us turn back."

CHAPTER 34

Yonkers had no news. Hastings none. But at Dobbs Ferry a motorcycle policeman reported to Valcour that he had chased a car that had cut off suddenly in the direction of Elmsford. The policeman had not got near enough to the car to get either its number or to make out its appearance. It might have been a roadster. It was a powerful car, and it was going like a bat out of hell.

Valcour studied a map. From Elmsford it was possible to swing north by way of Briarcliff to Amawalk and then west to the Hudson River at Peekskill, or they could have gone by way of Mt. Kisco, through Sodom up to Millerton, and then west to join the Albany road at Red Hook.

He hunted up a telephone booth and called headquarters. The consolidation of their reports to date centered on a roadster that had flashed through Kitchawan at a problematic speed of about seventy miles an hour. The local constable had shouted and had fired one shot in the air from his revolver. He had telephoned on ahead to Amawalk, and reported the reckless driving. Headquarters had picked up the report from Amawalk. That had been fifteen minutes ago. Amawalk had not yet reported the car.

Valcour hung up. He hurried to the commissioner's car and said to the driver, "Elmsford, and the Lake Mahopac road." Gears meshed and the car shot forward, cutting the hard white road with its powerful lights.

The commissioner lowered a window and tossed out the butt of a cigar. Wind whipped it as a streak of red fire to the rear. "This absurd mystification!" he said.

"You have confidence in me, Commissioner?"

"All in the world, my dear Valcour."

"I can perhaps explain things to you better after Amawalk."

"And what is Amawalk?"

"There is a motorcycle patrolman there, waiting."

"For our birds?"

"Yes. They've either got to go through Amawalk or back through Kitchawan. If they try that, they'll be stopped at Kitchawan."

"Then they are pocketed?"

"Practically. Of course there are some unimproved roads, but I believe they will stick to the cement. There is only one trouble."

"The world is filled with it. What's this one?"

"It is only six miles from Kitchawan to Amawalk, and the roadster was reported going through Kitchawan at a speed of seventy miles an hour over fifteen minutes ago. The trouble is, it has not as yet reached Amawalk." Valcour added quietly. "I think we are too late."

"They're off on byroads?"

"No, Commissioner. I think that one of those two young men is dead."

Elmsford shot at them. They kept straight ahead through four corners and then bore right on the concrete. The lights of a garage were brilliant. Were gone. The wooded road stretched clear, and the commissioner lighted another cigar.

It wasn't smart-aleckism, he knew, this silence on Valcour's part. There was a definite purpose behind it. What was there waiting for them between Kitchawan and Amawalk? The names irritated him. There was an amateurish woodsiness about them—fat business men haunched about camp fires. They should have been buried, those names, with the pioneers. Buried. Kate. Little Kate was dead on a bed, and the Police Commissioner of New York City was chasing her son.

They forked to the left across a small bridge, then on through four corners, and Briarcliff soon flashed past.

"About seven miles, now, to Kitchawan," Valcour said.

The commissioner did not hear. There was a private voice. Kate's voice, saying again to him: "We never stay very long in the same places... We are a good deal abroad, John, in the odder corners... Our life is quite simple, quite quiet... And after that? Just on and on." Every word of it was clear to him, and the scent of violets drifting from sealskin cut hesitantly through tobacco, and Valcour was giving him something. He stared at it incuriously. A small gold locket. Then his eyes were sharp with remembrance.

"I found it," Valcour said, "among the things in her handbag. It seemed advisable to keep it and to give it to you. Your photograph is in it."

"I know." He did not open the locket. Its cold and friendless metal warmed slowly in the fierce pressure of his hand. It was astonishing to keep a thing for forty years. To keep a thing intimately, as this thing must have been kept. And as it would continue to be kept.

A motorcycle roared behind, pressed up, and overtook them. The officer driving it recognized the car, the commissioner, saluted, and fell back. They forked to the left, and Valcour picked up the speaking tube. He said in it: "We strike Kitchawan in three miles. Stop there for reports and instructions."

The driver nodded. The car shot forward with increased speed, and four minutes later its powerful brakes brought it down to an evenly graduated stop. Valcour lowered a window and said to a goggled patrolman who had run alongside, "Any trace?"

"No, sir. The roadster hasn't returned this way and Amawalk just telephoned that there's nothing doing at their end yet. The car must have stopped somewhere in between, or taken a dirt road. Want me to go on with you?"

"No. Stay here."

"Yes, sir."

Valcour instructed their driver to go ahead slowly and to stop at each intersection or crossroad. The searchlight, controlled from the driver's seat, was to be kept on, and alternately to sweep each side of the road.

The car moved forward and soon to the left across a long bridge. At fifteen miles an hour it went, its searchlight cutting great swathes of white through the hedgerows and trees. A little over a mile from the bridge their route switched sharp to a road on the right.

The car stopped and Valcour got out. He examined the dirt continuation of the road along which they had been traveling. Deep tread marks of an expensive brand of tires were clearly plain.

"They've gone up here," he said.

The roadster was in darkness when they pulled alongside of it. Wilbur Strange was sitting behind the wheel, his legs stretched out, his hands clasped behind his head, staring up at the stars. His torpid body was heavy on the leather seat. Salt streaks down his face glistened wet. Henry was on the seat beside him. Henry was dead.

The commissioner nodded toward Wilbur. "Your murderer, Valcour?" he said.

Valcour withdrew the blinding flashlight from in front of Henry's dilated, staring dead eyes. "No, Commissioner. The murderer is still in the city house."

CHAPTER 35

The commissioner looked at him fixedly. "You are a curious man, Valcour. I have never known you to act like this before." Valcour was evasive. "It is a curious case," he said.

"You are in no doubt as to its solution?"

"None." Valcour deliberately sheered off. "Can you arrange things with the county authorities, Commissioner?"

"In what way?"

"To have Mr. Strange released into our custody, and to get permission from them to have the body brought back with us to town."

"Yes."… That lump of dead clay there on the seat was Kate's son.

"Then if you will permit me to suggest that you drive back to Kitchawan and do so? Perhaps you will also inform headquarters that the car has been found, and that the general alarm can be canceled? I will wait for you here with Mr. Strange. I want to look for a single piece of evidence. It is the only one that we need. If it is not in the car, or on the body, I will have to look for it along the road."

"What is it?"

"A silver flask, Commissioner. A small silver flask."

The Commissioner took another look at that death-varnished face. There was no Kate in it at all. It was all Willett. He got into his car, heavily, slowly. Its driver backed it, found a turning place, and its tail light vanished around a curve in the road.

They were in darkness. Valcour reached over to the roadster's instrument panel and switched on the panel light and the headlights.

"Did you notice the small silver flask that I have been speaking about, Mr. Strange?"

"No, Mr. Valcour."

Wilbur's voice was miserably thick and broken. His wet, unhappy eyes still stared above clasped hands at stars. His body seemed as drained of life as Henry's dead one on the leather seat beside him.

"Would you mind sitting on the running board, please?"

"Not at all, Mr. Valcour."

Wilbur unclasped his hands. His arms were numb from having kept them there so long. He flexed his muscles listlessly and opened the roadster's door. He got his legs outside and stood still for a moment leaning against the side of the car. "Can I help you?" he said.

"Thank you, no."

Wilbur walked to the other side of the road. He stretched flat on his stomach on the damp cool grass. His cold wet cheek pressed hard on the dew-drenched grass.

Valcour's flashlight explored the floor board of the car. Under Henry's awkwardly twisted feet it gleamed on silver. He moved the feet and very carefully picked up the small silver flask by the milled edge of its cap. He felt in his pocket and found an envelope. The flask fitted into it easily, and he put it in a breast pocket.

He switched off the panel lamp and Henry's slumped, placid face no longer looked unearthly from its glow. He walked across the dark roadway and sat down close to Wilbur's heavy and utterly lax body. "You are an odd youngster," he said. "I hope that you will consider me, in the future, as a friend."

Wilbur's cheek stayed pressed close on the grass. "You don't know, Mr. Valcour," he said.

"That college business? I think I do. The dean was extremely reticent when my man questioned him about it. He would go no further than implications, vague generalities."

"He was right about it. He was all right."

"He has never been convinced of the correctness of the course which he took. He felt that he had evaded, or missed, a responsibility. He has had qualms about it. He knew you, you see, Mr. Strange. Better than I did." Valcour added quietly: "He knew your history."

"Not much of a history."

"No, it wasn't. Nor especially unique. But you are unique." Valcour lighted a cigarette. "Care for one?"

"No, thank you."

Smoke was slowly drifting up in the air and Valcour said casually, "She must have been an extraordinary woman."

"His mother?"

"Yes."

"She did things for me."

"So I understand."

"She put me through college with her son. We roomed together." The voice was drifting along the grass, clinging along the dew-wet grass. "We did things together. We were pretty wild. Some of the things we did weren't nice. Need I be more explicit, Mr. Valcour?"

"No. I know."

"She took sick when she learned about it, after we resigned from college. The doctor said she died of some sort of anemia. They said it dilated her heart. I knew what it was. It wasn't diseased, Mr. Valcour. It was broken. He jumped out of a window. I went to prison. Not your kind of a prison, Mr. Valcour. The prison was inside of me."

"And then you put that remarkable advertisement in the papers."

A small wind passed above them through the trees, and tired leaves dropped reluctantly to the earth.

"Some people just naturally gravitate to misfortune, Mr. Valcour, don't you think?"

"How old were you then, Mr. Strange?"

"Eighteen."

Valcour's kindly eyes were unnaturally bright. "Someday," he said, "men who are as old as I am may have the God-given sense to remember what it was like to be eighteen. We forget, as life dulls us, the bright and chivalric metal that time and a world filled with disillusions have blackened with their tarnish." It suddenly occurred to him that Wilbur did not know of Mrs. Willett's death. He said it directly: "Mrs. Willett is dead."

"Then she knows about Henry. He's with her. She has him now."

"That's right, Mr. Strange. She has him now." He said with unaccustomed harshness: "You'd better get up off that wet grass or you'll get pneumonia."

Wilbur felt of the grass's wetness. "All right," he said.

He sat up.

"Tell me what happened to Henry.'

"There isn't much to tell, Mr. Valcour. You know how willful he was. The police supervision at the city house was getting on his nerves. He used to go a little crazy when things got on his nerves. He told me, after he came back upstairs from taking tea with his mother, that he was going to get the car out and beat it until the investigation was over. He had it fixed in his head that he could go up to camp until things in the city were over."

"Couldn't you stop him?"

"It wasn't ever wise to stop Henry when he had his mind set on a thing, until he'd cooled down. He'd do queer things to get his way. He told me this time that he'd be a beast to his mother if I didn't let him go. He would have been, too, Mr. Valcour. I went with him to bring him back. Later in the evening, after he'd cooled off a bit, I could have brought him back. His blood was sort of funny that way. It would get hot and make him do things. Arthur was like that."

"What happened after you left the house?"

"Henry drove pretty wild after we got out of the city and up past Yonkers. A motorcycle policeman almost caught us once. We didn't stop until we got up on this side road here."

"What did you do here?"

"I don't know. I mean, Mr. Valcour, I don't know what killed Henry. We walked for a while after we got out of the car. Henry said he wanted to stretch his legs. I thought it would get him cooled down enough, and I could take him home. We started for the car and almost reached it when Henry said he'd dropped his hat and told me to go back and get it. I did walk back along the road. I hadn't any flashlight. I struck matches. I couldn't find the hat, and went back to the car. Henry was sitting the way you found him. I thought he was kidding. I knew he wasn't asleep, because his eyes were open. Then I knew he was dead."

"What did you do?"

"I got in and sat down beside him." Wilbur was still for a while. Then he said: "Do you know what killed him, Mr. Valcour?"

"I believe it was the same poison that killed Mrs. Willett. Aconite."

Lights flashed full on them from around a curve, and the commissioner's car drew swiftly alongside and came to a stop. The commissioner got out.

"I have had a bad time of it, Valcour," he said. "I think that if all the red tape that had to be slashed through were laid end to end—well, pick your own terminal points for them, but make them far apart."

"Everything arranged, Commissioner?"

"Yes. Find the flask?"

"I have it."

"How are we going to fix things up?" The commissioner stared toward the slumped body of Kate's dead son. She wouldn't want him left sitting that way. "If you will help me, Valcour," he said.

His driver stepped forward. "Let me do this, sir."

"Thank you. I will attend to it myself." He lifted, with Valcour, Kate's dead boy from the roadster. It was loose and heavy between them as they carried the body to the limousine. It was not uncomfortable-looking, stretched on the rear scat of the car's broad tonneau. "Isn't it wise—don't they tie a handkerchief under the chin, Valcour?"

"Yes, Commissioner."

"Thank you, I have one." His fingers were clumsy as they tied the knot.

"I wouldn't put a cushion under the head, Commissioner."

"That's right, Valcour. We'd better not." He closed the lids over staring eyes. "If we drive slowly?"

"I could sit on the floor," Wilbur said. "He wouldn't move."

"All right, Mr. Strange. You will drive carefully, Valcour? I will ride with you in front." He turned to his driver and said: "You will follow us in the roadster."

There was a dignity to it, the quiet and careful passage back through Westchester, the official siren stilled, the silent passage through the city, down to the brownstone house with its substantial and ugly face upon the park.

They carried Henry in and onto a sofa in the long and narrow drawing room, and Valcour walked slowly up the broad oak stairs. The man stationed as a guard for that floor met him at their head.

"I wouldn't let him go inside, Lieutenant," he said. "But I didn't have the heart in me to stop him from doing that."

Valcour looked past the man's shoulder to the end of the hall. To Mrs. Willett's door. Larry was sitting on a chair beside it and loosely heaped, pressed to its base, were roses.

CHAPTER 36

Valcour kept his voice low. He said to the patrolman: "I understand that the medical examiner is still here. I believe you will find him in the library. Will you look him up, please, and ask him to join me in Mrs. Willett's room?"

"Yes, sir."

The patrolman started downstairs, and Larry stood up as Valcour walked toward him.

"Will it be all right to go in now?"

"In a few minutes, Mr. Stone. There is a short conference I must have in there with the medical examiner. There are still several things to do. I will call you."

"Thank you, Mr. Valcour."

Valcour did not open the door. He looked at Larry and said, "Will you explain to me, please, about that twenty thousand dollars? Was it Arthur or Henry? You see, Mr. Stone, it can't matter to Mrs. Willett now."

The phrase was a slow muddy river in Larry's miserable head: it can't matter to her now. Nothing—ever—could matter again to Kate. "Arthur took it, Mr. Valcour," he said. "He took it from her dresser up in camp."—That dresser, before whose mirror Kate must have sat and sat during those bitter, solitary hours, and found God Himself alone knew what souvenirs of wastedness looking back at her from naked eyes.—"I didn't know until later what it was he'd taken. When I knew, and after I'd found the spot where he'd hidden it, it was too late. Kate knew of the theft by then. But she didn't know the thief. I think it hurt her least for me to be the thief."

"You misjudge her, Mr. Stone. Mrs. Willett was an unusually understanding woman. I am certain that she deliberately blinded herself concerning the theft of that money, beyond a conviction in the utter impossibility of your guilt."

"I am glad if that is so."

Valcour went into the room and closed the door. A sheet covered Mrs. Willett's body completely. He went to a bureau and picked up a hand mirror. He went over to the great mahogany bed and exposed one arm and one hand. He did things with the mirror, and replaced the sheet.

He sat down at the tea table and snapped on a standing lamp that was beside it. He was busied for five minutes beneath its strong white light. The door opened, closed, and the medical examiner came over toward him. "You wanted to see me, Valcour?"

"If you please, Doctor. You have examined the body of Henry Willett?"

"Superficially. Aconite again, I should say. The same as with Mrs. Willett."

"Would you be good enough to test this with the tip of your tongue?" Valcour carefully unscrewed the lid from the little silver flask. "If you will hold it, please, by its edges without permitting your fingers to touch the body of the flask? Thank you."

"Yes—the whiskey makes it hard to tell, of course. I should say there was aconite in it. A strong dose."

Valcour was silent for a moment. "Doctor, will it be possible to waive holding an autopsy on Mrs. Willett?"

"That's a queer thing for you to say, Valcour."

"I know it. But consider, please, the following points: both Dr. Stiernheim's opinion and your own coincide to the effect that death was caused by an overdose of aconite. There is aconite in the tea dregs of the cup from which Mrs. Willett was drinking immediately before her death."

"All perfectly true, but why not hold an autopsy?"

"Because I think that not to do so would please the commissioner very much."

The medical examiner said carefully, "I see." He didn't.

"The commissioner and Mrs. Willett were friends as children. I have the impression that at some time during their early lives they were fond of one another."

"I sec."

"Lastly, Doctor, not to do so would in no way balk justice. There is no question as to the identity of the perpetrator of these crimes."

"You know that?"

"I know it, and I have proof.'"

"Who is it?"

"If you will forgive me, I must first confer with the commissioner."

"Well, Valcour—of course it could be done. If the commissioner will personally request me to waive an autopsy, I shall do so."

"That is kind of you, Doctor. He will request it."

"Anything further?"

"Mrs. Willett's nephew is sitting in the hallway by the door. He would be grateful to you for permission to place some flowers here in the room, possibly on the bed. You are finished with the body?"

"Quite. I shall speak to the commissioner myself about that autopsy business on my way out. I dare say that an undertaker can then take charge."

Valcour accompanied the medical examiner to the door. He opened it and waited until the doctor had gone on down the hall, then he said, "If you care to bring those flowers in now, Mr. Stone, it will be quite all right. I regret that I cannot as yet turn the room over to the family entirely. That can only be done after I have had a short talk with the commissioner."

Valcour went back to the tea table, and sat there, not facing Larry, while the flowers were arranged.

"There is no objection to uncovering her face, Mr. Valcour?"

"None at all, Mr. Stone."

"It looks smothered."

The air in the room was thickening with the scent of roses. There must have been, Valcour thought, dozens on dozens of them, and their fragrance was heavy with every breath. He felt it was odd that the most beautiful and tranquil moments of one's stay on earth should be spent when one was freshly dead. Those few short hours between life's ending and the grave, in which were crushed such a wealth of heart-breaking love, such a nakedness of love, that had been hidden so torpidly in those who were left, and whom one had cared for so, until one had ceased to breathe. He busied himself with jotting down meaningless notes on a piece of paper until Larry had finished, then he said: "Will you do me a favor, please, Mr. Stone?"

"Certainly."

"Will you locate the commissioner and ask him to join me up here?" Valcour stood up. He watched Larry walking toward the door. He said to him as he reached it, "Before you go, tell me one thing."

"Yes, Mr. Valcour?"

"On the morning of the day of Arthur's murder up in camp, when you snatched that gun from Linda Willett's hand and pushed her so that she struck her shoulder against the opposite wall of the hallway, why did you drop the matter there?"

Larry said dully, "She recognized me?"

"No, Mr. Stone. But she caught sight of your hair. I could eliminate Mr. Strange because his hair is black. As for Jess Willett, he would have come right out into the hall and confronted her. And neither Henry nor Arthur would have had the intelligence to comprehend her intention, or the flexibility of brain power to have acted so quickly. That left you. Did she have the muzzle of the gun in her mouth?"

"She was about to pull the trigger."

CHAPTER 37

"Well, Valcour, you are ready to make an arrest?"

Valcour's voice was peculiar. "Sit down, Commissioner," he said.

The commissioner paused, on his way over to the tea table, at the foot of the bed. He stared hard at Mrs. Willett. At Kate. Her silver hair and pale face peaceful among roses.

"I am glad that she is out of all this at last," he said. He picked up a flower that had fallen to the floor. He did not replace it with the others heaped so extravagantly on the broad white sheet. He carried it over with him to the tea table and sat down. "What are all of these things?"

"Our evidence. I prefer, before we take any action, to go over the case with you."

"But is this delay wise, Valcour?"

"The criminal is well guarded."

"Then begin."

"I have delayed until this moment, so that the case would be proven to our satisfaction beyond the shadow of a doubt."

"Name the criminal, Valcour."

"Permit me, Commissioner. I am not devious without a purpose. We will go back to last August when the first machinery for the accomplishment of these crimes was put into operation. The threat notes. I know now definitely that the criminal was intimately aware of each movement of the Willett family and had the opportunity to address and to send them correctly, as well as to conceive and execute that rather clever business of the final one, which arrived in our hands as a blank sheet of paper. I will return to its envelope later."

"You know the motive for them, Valcour?"

"I do."

"Money?"

"Not money."

"Well?"

"We will come to it."

"As you wish." The rose in his hand was not more fragrant than the air in the room itself.

"The criminal had the opportunity up at camp for getting the target rifle and using it to shoot Arthur, then throwing it after the crime from a bedroom window to the spot on the path where it was later found by Mr. Stone.

"Let me recall that message which Slade sent to you while we were down in Bermuda. I have a copy of it here. I will read it to you." Valcour picked up a sheet of paper from the table and read: "'Sir—My conscience compels me to inform you that I withheld, at the inquest, information strongly pointing toward the person who shot and killed Mr. Arthur Willett. I saw that person passing through the kitchen door that opens into the central hallway, at what must have been but a brief moment after the commission of the crime. I had myself just entered my bedroom, after having gotten a box of bicarbonate of soda which was on a shelf above the kitchen sink, and its door was ajar. I waited, at the inquest, for that person to speak. I tried by my testimony to compel that person to speak—"

"Linda!" the commissioner broke in.

"No, not Linda. Let me conclude the message: 'I will wait until after the family returns from Bermuda, and will then ask that person to confess, for in such fashion can one's soul best be purged of its sin and again be made acceptable to our Lord. But if no confession is forthcoming, I shall consider it my duty both before God and before man to speak myself. I am sir, respectfully your humble servant, William Slade.'" Valcour put the paper back upon the table. "Slade verified his suspicions. Commissioner, to-day. When it came to the point of disclosing them to us, he could not do so. He preferred to kill himself instead."

"You have proof of it?"

"I have. Let us now take the deaths of Mrs. Willett and of Henry. The opportunity was present to the criminal in each case, both to put the aconite in that cup of tea, and into the silver flask that was carried by Henry on to-night's ride. That flask is one of a pair." Valcour indicated a miniature silver tantalus on the table. A small flask, the mate to the one that had been carried by Henry, was still in it. "The fingerprints of the criminal are the only ones to be found on the flat silver rim at the bottom of that tantalus. They are also the only fingerprints to be found on that half-emptied bottle of tincture of aconite which you see standing beside it."

"Valcour, you have previously eliminated Wilbur Strange, but if this flask was carried by Henry, why was there not a chance that Mr. Strange would have taken a drink from it, too?"

"Really none, Commissioner. You see how small it is. There isn't more than one good-sized drink in it. The criminal knew Henry's character and his habits very well. There wasn't a chance in a hundred that Henry would have used one drop of that flask's contents for anyone but himself. Let us turn next to these two books. One has a yellow jacket, and the other one a blue. They are patently dissimilar. After the tea tray was brought in here this afternoon, Mrs. Willett told Simpson to go upstairs and ask Henry to come down and join her. Mrs. Willett was sitting in the chair you arc occupying now, and the yellow-jacketed book was in her hand. When Simpson returned, Mrs. Willett was still sitting as when Simpson had left her, but she no longer had the yellow-jacketed book. She had, instead, the blue one. We can presume from this that during Simpson's absence Mrs. Willett got out of her chair and went—as the yellow-jacketed book was found in it—into the bathroom. Simpson was gone not over three minutes in all, but during that time the aconite was put in Mrs. Willett's teacup."

"But what was the motive for all this, Valcour?"

"Henry—Arthur—you know them. Without someone who loved them very much, life would be most unkind to them. They were a vicious burden on the family. They warped it, and forced it to live abnormally. They would develop in their later and pitiful years into being a burden upon themselves. There was a decided trend toward megalomania, with the future dreaded possibility of incarceration in some institution for the mentally diseased. It was an act of love to kill them. They were better dead."

"And why kill Kate?"

Valcour gently opened an enamel compact lying among the things on the table. "This face powder and this rouge, Commissioner, left their trace upon the wood stock of that target rifle up at camp. Simpson saw this little silver flask, which contains the poison and which has the criminal's fingerprints upon it, being slipped this afternoon into Henry's pocket. I checked those fingerprints myself upon our return here to the house tonight. It was certain, you see, that Henry and Henry alone would drink the flask's contents. This cablegram which Slade sent to Bermuda states, not that the city house was opened, but that he intended upon our return to tell what he knew. This revolver, the tantalus, the bottle of aconite, I found hidden among the plumbing of the bathtub in the bathroom connecting with this room. I think you can understand now, Commissioner, why I wanted to be very certain of my facts before I spoke. For the same fingerprints that are on this little flask are also on that locket by your heart."

The commissioner was on his feet.

"Kate," he said, while old age filled him. "My little Kate."

Printed in Great Britain
by Amazon

16876571R00089